meet me at the convenience store by the sea

meet me at the convenience store by the sea

sonoko machida
translated by bruno navasky

ORION

First published in Japanese as *Konbini Kyodai Vol 2: Tenderness Moji-Ko Koganemura-ten* in 2022. English translation rights arranged with SHINCHOSHA Publishing Co., Ltd., Tokyo, in care of Tuttle-Mori Agency, Inc., Tokyo.

An Orion Paperback

First published in Great Britain in 2026 by Orion Fiction,
an imprint of The Orion Publishing Group Ltd.
Carmelite House, 50 Victoria Embankment
London EC4Y 0DZ

An Hachette UK Company

1 3 5 7 9 10 8 6 4 2

Copyright © Sonoko Machida 2022
English translation © Bruno Navasky 2026
Interior illustrations © Saskia Leboff

The moral right of Sonoko Machida to be identified as the author of this work has been asserted in accordance with the Copyright, Designs and Patents Act of 1988.

Bruno Navasky has asserted his right to be identified as the translator of this work.

All rights reserved. No part of this publication may be reproduced, stored in a retrieval system, or transmitted in any form or by any means, electronic, mechanical, photocopying, recording, or otherwise, without the prior permission of both the copyright owner and the above publisher of this book.

All the characters in this book are fictitious, and any resemblance to actual persons, living or dead, is purely coincidental.

A CIP catalogue record for this book is
available from the British Library.

ISBN (Mass Market Paperback) 978 139 872 879 0
ISBN (Ebook) 978 139 872 880 6
ISBN (Audio) 978 139 872 881 3

Typeset by Born Group
Printed and bound in Great Britain by Clays Ltd, Elcograf S.p.A.

www.orionbooks.co.uk

Cast of Characters
An Introduction

Mitsuhiko Shiba ('Mitsu')
The beloved and strangely attractive manager of the Tenderness Koganemura, an outpost of a chain of local convenience stores operating in Kyushu, an island in Japan.

Nihiko Shiba ('Tsugi')
Brother to Mitsu and man of mystery who frequents the Tenderness Koganemura store. Wears a coverall with 'Whatever Guy' printed on it.

Jewel Shiba
Youngest of the five Shiba siblings, she's an office worker in the same building as the Tenderness store and possesses a beauty that rivals her brother Mitsu's.

Tarō Hirose
Part-time employee at the Tenderness.

Old Red
The self-styled 'Mojikō Tourism Ambassador', he wears bright red overalls and rides around on a three-wheel cargo bike. His quirky appearance has made him a household name in Mojikō.

About Tenderness

Tenderness is a convenience store chain operating only in Kyushu.

With the motto 'Caring for People, Caring for you = Tenderness,' the chain pays close attention to the well-being of their customers, serving bentō box meals and sweets emphasising local colour and flavours. Despite its small size, the Mojikō Koganemura branch in particular is one of its premier locations, thanks to the tireless effort and devotion of its manager, and the patronage of his many admirers.

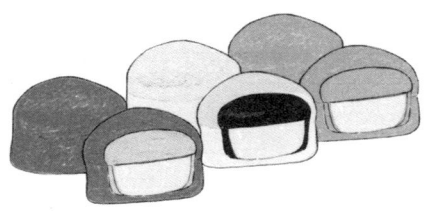

Prologue

'I want to go to Mojikō . . .'
It was the end of term at university and the teen boutique where I worked part-time was closed for the Obon festival. Lounging around the house with nothing to do, I sprawled on my beanbag talking to myself.
'I want to go to Mojikō . . .'
About three months ago, I had taken my brand new car – I call her Pipienne – out for a ride, and happened to find myself in Mojikō for the very first time. I had never given Mojikō much thought, but after a few hours there, I fell totally in love with the place. Cute retro buildings dotting the landscape between the mountains and the sea, small side-streets bustling with people, delicious treats around every corner. It was like visiting another country.
And then, that convenience store. The Tenderness at the Golden Villa apartments.
I've been to stores in all sorts of places since then, but none of them have captivated me the way this one did. You can buy Tenderness products all over Kyushu, but there was

something about the Golden Villa Tenderness in Mojikō. Maybe it had something to do with the store manager.

'Please come back soon!' he had said, smiling. I couldn't get it out of my head.

'I want to go to Mojikō . . .'

I was talking out loud, saying it for the zillionth time, when suddenly there was a whack on my head.

'Ow! What?!'

I looked up. My friend Makio Tsuruta stood in front of me, hands on his hips. Makio and I have been friends forever – we're like family.

'What are you babbling about?' he asked.

'Huh? Oh, hi Makio. What's up?'

'What's up? I've been parked by your front door forever, shouting hello, but no one answered. That's what's up.'

'Oops. My parents are out right now.'

'Yes, I can see that. And you're lying around babbling about Mojikō. Waka, at least answer the door. Anyway, here. These are from my mum,' he said, handing me a Tupperware full of *ikinari dango* – his mother's steamed rice buns.

Ikinari dango are a speciality of Kumamoto, our neighbourhood, and the ones Makio's mother makes are so good I could cry. They're pro level – she could open a store, they're that good, but she just makes them as a hobby, which is kind of a shame.

I popped open the Tupperware right away and bit into one. It was delicious – tender, crumbly sweet-potato filling and luscious red bean paste, sweet but not too sweet, wrapped in a slightly stretchy rice-flour skin, perfectly chewy, exquisite as always.

'Yum! So good. But, Makio . . . Don't you have anything better to do?' I snorted a little, wondering why a third-year university student was running errands for his mother.

'I don't need to hear that from a babbling couch potato,' he retorted. Which was fair enough. 'I mean, why Mojikō?' he asked. 'That's in North Kyushu, isn't it? Why do you want to go to the middle of nowhere?'

Makio gave me a quizzical look, and I got a little mad.

'The middle of nowhere? People shouldn't comment on things they know nothing about! Mojikō is great!' I told him all about my little trip there three months ago, and all the good things I had found, and declared, 'I think it's awesome, anyway. And I want to go.'

'So why don't you?'

'I want to! But Pipienne . . . poor Pipienne . . .'

Two months ago, I had driven my beloved car Pipienne into our family rice paddy. I was driving home, humming a happy tune, when all of a sudden a little white cat jumped in front of the car, and I had to yank the steering wheel to one side. Part of the rice paddy was ruined, too, and the cost to tow and repair Pipienne was insane. The white cat may have turned out to be just a plastic bag. But at least I wasn't hurt at all.

My dad was so furious that the rice he had been labouring over for most of the year had been ruined that I lost custody of Pipienne. She's back home from the mechanic now, but she just sits in the barn, gathering dust.

'You were there for Pipienne's rescue mission, weren't you? No matter how much I want to go, I can't!'

'Hmm,' Makio said. He thought for a second, then said, 'Okay, Waka, why don't I take you? I want to take a look at this Mojikō that you're so in love with, see what it's like. If you don't mind me tagging along, I'll drive you there.'

I had completely forgotten that Makio had a car of his own – his father's old Honda Civic. It was the deep maroon colour of a sweet red azuki bean, so of course I had nicknamed it 'Azuki'.

'Azuki's air conditioning is a little weak, isn't it?' I joked.

'Okay, forget it,' said Makio. 'I won't take you.'

'I'll go, I'll go!' I laughed.

So we were off to Mojikō, the land of my dreams.

It had been a while, but the atmosphere was as pleasant as ever. The sky and sea were bright blue and the sea breeze felt good on my skin. Even Makio forgot to make fun of it being the middle of nowhere.

'It's a great spot, isn't it?' I said. 'Look over there! They even have rickshaws!'

'It is pretty cool,' he admitted. 'Not thanks to me or anything, but still.'

I had eaten the famous baked curry au gratin the last time I was here, but I had looked it up after I got home and discovered that each shop had its own secret recipe. So we went to try one of the other restaurants that I had noticed, but there was a surprisingly long line. We agreed that must mean it was really good, and we queued up.

'It's warm here. But it's cool to eat hot things when it's hot.'

'Makio, you really get it, don't you?' I clapped my hands in delight. 'But let's go for ice cream after, okay?'

'Oh, for sure,' he replied. 'Ice cream in a place like this has got to be good.'

We ate the baked curry, sweat rolling down our faces, then took a stroll around the neighbourhood, lapping up ice cream as we walked. There was a sightseeing trolley that looked like it might be for tourists, so we got on. The trolley rattled slowly along, full of people, mostly parents with small children. Riding among them with Makio gave me a funny feeling. We had ridden on all sorts of vehicles like this, clinging to each other, when we were little kids. We had even slept in the same bed when our families holidayed together.

'It feels kind of nostalgic, doesn't it?' I asked suddenly, and Makio nodded.

'Mm. The stores, the streets, all that. Nostalgic.'

'It's not all brand new – there are old-fashioned things here, too. I like that.'

'Yup. Feels good.'

Makio and I never needed to say much to understand each other. Childhood friends are good like that.

I giggled a little and Makio gave me a light nudge. 'You're smiling! You like hanging out with me, don't you?'

'I was just thinking how nice it is to have a childhood friend,' I said.

'Oh. Right. Yeah, it's pretty nice . . .'

'Anyway, I'm thirsty. That curry was spicy.'

'Yeah, I guess. We can get something to drink when we get off the trolley. There's got to be a convenience store around here somewhere.'

Makio's words reminded me that I was here for a reason. My big goal in coming to Mojikō was to visit the Tenderness shop at Golden Villa.

'Makio! Let's get off here. I know a place!'

I grabbed his arm and Makio said, 'Oh? Okay, sure.' He seemed flustered, somehow.

We jumped off the trolley and, relying on my memory, headed off towards the Golden Villa Tenderness. The street that I had walked down so casually a few months before seemed to be shining brightly, as if it were welcoming me back.

'Hey, here's a store. What about this one?'

'Nope. A little further!' I said.

Makio followed along behind me, looking a little doubtful as I ploughed briskly forward. The sunlight was strong, and I was sweating quite a bit at this point, but I couldn't stop. Would he be there? I hoped so with every fibre of my being. He had to be!

The signpost of the Tenderness popped into view. As the emblem of his store, it suddenly seemed even more precious to me than my own family crest. It felt like a fanfare of trumpets was blaring in my head.

'There!'

Unable to stop myself, I broke into a trot. I had a vague sense of Makio running after me, calling out, 'What's going on?'

I ran straight through the car park and charged into the store. The familiar entrance melody rang out.

'Welcome!'

The same gentle voice, caressing my ears. There was no mistaking it. It was him!

I looked around. There he stood, smiling calmly at the checkout counter.

'Whoa. He's handsome.' I could hear Makio muttering behind me, but the words sounded far away in the distance somewhere.

Yes, this was it. Now I knew for sure. I had fallen in love with him. During that briefest of encounters, three months ago.

'C'mon, Waka, let's get some tea!'

Even as Makio spoke, I was running towards the counter. Watching me sprint towards him so quickly like that, the manager looked a little surprised, but smiled like he understood somehow.

Oh, don't smile like that – I can't take it! Just that simple smile made me feel like he knew we were fated to be.

'Hi! My name is Oishi Waka! What's yours?'

There was no time for hesitation, no room for embarrassment. The distance between us was too great – I had to close the gap somehow.

He blinked slightly, and then, in his sweet, sweet voice, the man said, 'I'm Shiba Mitsuhiko. I'm the store manager.'

'Mr Shiba . . .'

'Yes?'

He smiled. A smile straight and true, aimed right at me, and just thinking about it made me sure I was about to get a nosebleed. All my life, whenever I get too excited, my nose starts to bleed. So I quickly lifted my chin, just in case.

'Is something wrong?'

'N-no! Thank you!'

There was no way I was going to let him see me with a bloody nose. But I could definitely feel it starting, so I ran outside, pinching my nose tight. I dashed to a hidden corner of the car park, out of view of the counter, and sat down. I let go of my nose and looked down, and the instant I did, there it was – a drop of bright red blood.

'I've got it bad. Real bad,' I mumbled to myself. I'm not a wordsmith at the best of times, but now all my words had vanished.

'Hey! Waka!'

Makio was calling me. I looked up. He came running up, holding two bottles of cold tea. Seeing the state of me, he set them down, quickly pulled a pack of tissues from his pocket and handed one to me.

'I was going to ask you what's wrong, but I think I get it. You're into that guy in the store, aren't you?'

Makio sounded a little astonished.

I wiped my nose with the tissue. 'Yeah,' I admitted. 'I think I really like him. It's bad.'

'Nothing bad about it. Your nose always bleeds when you're with a guy you fancy. It's ridiculous,' he said.

He gave me one of the bottles. I took it with my free hand, and Makio took a long drink from the other bottle.

'But this time you picked someone out of your league. He's like the Manslayer from *Dragon Quest*.'

'Yeah, I know.'

'You have to choose someone closer to your level.'

'No,' I said, stuffing a tissue up my nose. 'Not a chance. I'll just level up. I'll figure it out. But that means I need to get Pipienne back right away. So I can come back to Mojikō. To see Mr Shiba!'

Mr Shiba. Such a beautiful name.

If I could be with him for just a few moments, I knew the distance between Kumamoto and Mojikō wouldn't matter to us.

As I made this declaration, Makio let out a sigh.

'Probably shouldn't have brought her,' he mumbled under his breath.

'Huh? What?'

'I should have just given you the dumplings and gone home.'

I had no idea what he was talking about, but Makio just went on muttering to himself.

'What's the use? I guess I'll have to live with it. Waka always sets her sights on the top prize, doesn't she?'

'Are you still going on about *Dragon Quest*? I mean, obviously, when it comes to the Quest, you don't settle for a unicorn rabbit when there are bigger prizes to win. You have to test the limits.'

When I said that, Makio had more to say that wasn't making much sense, like 'I wonder if the prizes themselves can level up, too?'

Whatever. If he wants to play *Dragon Quest* so bad, I'll lend him the game.

'Well, anyway,' Makio said. 'Drink your tea. Today's really just too hot.'

I did as I was told and put the bottle to my mouth. The cold, sweet tea slipped gently down.

'Ahh . . . that's good. Thank you, Makio.'

'Let's finish these and go home. Or did you want to try to go back into the store?'

I thought about it a little. I wanted to see Mr Shiba again, but I couldn't risk another nosebleed. I needed to build up some resistance. I wondered if there was a crash course in not getting nosebleeds when confronted by Mr Right?

'Let's call it a day. I need to go and do some research on nose exercises.'

'Well, that makes no sense at all.'

I looked up. The sky spread out above me, clear blue behind the brilliant white of the cumulonimbus clouds. Whenever I fall in love, my vision goes vivid like that, and the world takes on a beautiful glow. Right now, the world reflected in my eyes was as beautiful as it could possibly be.

'The season of love has begun,' I declared, and Makio grumbled.

'Oh man, this is gonna be rough.'

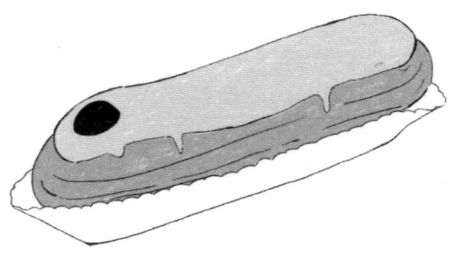

Chapter 1
On Love and Grandmothers

In the game of love, you have to save your progress frequently, or it's Game Over.

Shino Nagata had recently learned that this was the way of the world. When you sense trouble, you need to meet face-to-face or things will quickly go south. And it's absolutely essential to check your relationship status daily, particularly if your love score is low. Any little thing can happen, and in no time at all – Game Over.

People always talked about how adolescents were thin-skinned, but adolescent love – now, that was an infinitely more delicate thing. Shino had once seen a story online about the Mola mola, a fish said to be so sensitive that it frequently died in captivity. Love, she thought, was equally hard to sustain.

Shino's 'love' had come to an end after a mere two days home alone. She had eaten some bad red-clam sashimi, spent two days sick in bed and stumbled into school on the third day still feeling unsteady, only to find that her boyfriend, Daisuke Kanazawa, had dumped her, and all he had to say for himself was: 'There's a girl I like.'

Apparently, while Shino was absent, an older girl, a year above them, had told Daisuke he looked like her 'type'. They had swapped numbers, they got along really well and they had already kissed, he explained, which left Shino awash in a sea of questions.

'Were my two days really the same as your two days?'

It was so strange that if it were a book, Shino would assume they had printed the pages out of order. But Daisuke just stuck out his lower lip and said, 'Of course they were the same.'

Shino looked at him in confusion.

In other words, she thought, *while I was home miserable for two days, unable to contact him, my boyfriend wasn't worrying about me at all, but instead just switched to another girl?*

Shino wondered if there was something she had done wrong. Maybe she had been too slow to get physical with him? But they had kissed – just touching lips lightly, to be fair, nothing too serious, but wasn't that plenty for first-year high-school students? Going any further was a long way off. Shino didn't think she was ready for that, and besides, she had been warned time and again since middle school that if the worst came to the worst, it would always be the woman who would suffer. But she didn't like to think that Daisuke would break up with her over something like that. She'd rather imagine he'd had a fateful encounter, so powerful that he no longer cared at all about his bedridden girlfriend.

Not sure what to make of Shino, so deeply immersed in her thoughts, Daisuke bowed his head meekly and said,

'Sorry.' But then, just as quickly, he lifted it with an easy smile. 'It was pretty bad of me, wasn't it? But you'll be fine on your own, won't you, Shino?'

Shino's mouth fell open.

Was he really palming her off with such a lame line?

Daisuke definitely had an adolescent side to him, Shino had often thought. He liked to throw around big words like 'love' and 'eternity'. But still – had he really just said that?

Seeing Shino recoil at his words, Daisuke grimaced for a moment, then said, 'Well, Yukari needs me . . .' and ran off to take his place beside the new girlfriend, who had been secretly observing the whole conversation. Shino watched him go.

Meeting her shocked gaze with a sad frown, the new girl, Yukari, silently mouthed, 'Sorry.' Then she made a show of taking Daisuke firmly by the hand.

Shino and Daisuke had been dating since the spring of their third year in middle school. Daisuke had started things between them with a confession: 'I like you. As a girl.'

They had been classmates ever since primary school. It was natural that they had become close, and maybe for that reason, Shino could still distinctly recall the intense awkwardness of Daisuke's admission. She herself had harboured similar feelings towards him, but they had been too close for her to say anything about it.

'I want us to go to the same high school,' he'd said. 'We should stay together.'

Daisuke's grades weren't so good, and the high school that Shino had set her sights on seemed like a difficult reach for him. But she'd replied, 'Let's do it!' and they'd studied like mad, just the two of them. With her help, Daisuke eventually got the hang of things, his grades improved steadily and, as a result, the two of them were able to attend the same school after all. *So this is what 'smooth sailing' means*, Shino had thought happily, but she hadn't imagined that her happiness could be so fleeting.

Or, for that matter, that Daisuke's feelings could be so shallow. Watching Daisuke and Yukari go off hand in hand, she felt she had been cruelly mistreated.

Now she was just a minor character in another couple's love story. Just like that, Daisuke had thrown it all away – Shino, who had been with him since primary school, and everything they had been through together in this time. So he was that sort of person.

Whatever 'love' that had remained inside Shino was extinguished instantly. It was like when you get tired of a game app that you've been playing nonstop, so you just uninstall it. Along with embarrassment over having been so obsessed with a game like that in the first place, she felt a vague determination to stop wasting her time on such things. She was a little disappointed in herself, but also a little proud not to have lowered her sights when it came to her high-school ambitions, just to cater to Daisuke's academic shortcomings. In the end, she had resisted distorting her life for love, and that was worth something.

'Teenage love is like a cicada during its single summer on earth. It's born, makes a quick little buzz and then it's over before you can say *boo!*'

It was dinner time, two weeks after Shino and Daisuke had split up. When the voice came on their television, which was never turned off, Shino looked up with some interest from the bowl of keema curry she was eating. A heavily made-up older woman was doing the talking.

Cicadas. So teenage love was doomed from the start – was that how it was? It would be a new answer to her own recent concerns. Maybe it didn't make sense to obsess over 'saving the game'. But still . . .

'Cicadas, eh? That's saying something.'

Her father, Takao, spoke from across the table, where he was having his evening drink.

'Romance is no good for children. There are more important things to do with your time now. You understand that, Shino?'

Shino gave a perfunctory nod and glanced at the empty cans in front of her father. There were two. *Hm, not drunk yet*, she thought to herself.

'Young women in particular have no cause to be dating,' he continued. 'Listen now, if I heard you were seeing a young man, I wouldn't tolerate it. I'd have a few sharp words with the boy's parents, before there was trouble.'

'Dad, it's okay. Don't worry about it. I'm not seeing anyone, anyway.' Shino glumly put a spoonful of curry in her mouth.

'Good, good,' Takao said, letting a tolerant note creep into his voice. 'And let's keep it that way.'

'. . . And sex, with cicada love? Out of the question!' The woman on TV continued her tirade as Shino turned back to watch. 'With young people, it becomes a rollercoaster of sexual desire. They get all worked up, they think they like someone or love them, but ninety-nine per cent of it is hormones. It's actually old-fashioned, giving yourself over to lust when you're so immature. The idea that young people have to sow their seed so quickly belongs to another era, back when people died young. Let's make it clear: these days, sex between teenagers is unnecessary.'

'Ugh, gross,' Shino nearly said out loud. No matter what her point was, listening to a woman of that age talk about love and sex during dinner with her parents was too much. Besides, anything with a sexual theme was untouchable in the Nagata household. It was a taboo topic, to be discussed only with careful words like 'indiscretion' or 'faux pas' that would obscure any racy curves, leaving only a vague silhouette.

What would Papa do if he knew that I had kissed a boy so often? Shino wondered suddenly. Would he yell, or just stare at her with contempt? When they heard on TV that a teen idol had announced her shotgun wedding, he'd always say, 'Just shameless!' So maybe he'd call her shameless? But then, when the idol's teen-dad boyfriend declared, 'I'll take care of my wife and child no matter what,' Shino's father was full of approval: 'Well said, young man!'

If I were a boy, Shino thought, *and said that I had a girlfriend? He'd probably be impressed. Well, I guess that's just how it is, but still.*

As Shino mulled this over, the woman on TV kept repeating the word 'sex' as she spoke. Takao slammed his beer glass down on the table.

'Vulgar woman! There may be some truth to what she says, but it sounds like she's just aiming for shock value. Right, Yumi?'

Shino's mother, Yumi, was freshening Takao's drink. 'Yes, dear,' she replied absent-mindedly.

'I don't get it.' On TV, a loud girl wearing a name tag reading 'Yukihime (18 Years Old)' spoke sharply to the older woman. 'Teenagers know what love is. I mean, we love our children and all that, don't we?' The screen displayed a photo of her together with a young girl, so she must have been a teen mum. She had pink-beige hair, loud fingernails and wore a top that accentuated her cleavage.

'Listen, there's something wrong with this girl's parents.' A veneer of pity couldn't hide the note of superiority in Takao's voice. 'She wasn't raised right. She doesn't understand the risks of teen marriage and childbirth.'

'Yes, dear.'

Responding in the same tone as before, Yumi placed two small bowls in front of her husband. Glancing at their contents, Takao pushed one to the side and reached for the other with his chopsticks. He required snacks with his evening drink, but he had a long list of likes and dislikes, and some things he wouldn't touch.

Shino took a peek at the bowl Takao had pushed aside and noted that it was full of simmered vegetables. As a child, Shino had been scolded time and again not to be picky about what she ate, but Takao himself never seemed bound by such concerns.

'It's a vicious circle, see? Children raising children – that's a B-grade horror movie, there. Brrr . . .!' Takao gave an exaggerated shudder.

Shino said nothing and focused on polishing off her bowl of curry. She wanted to get back to her room as quickly as possible. The curry was a little spicy. Her mouth was prickling, but she crammed it in anyway.

'Thanks for dinner,' she said and stood up. She gathered her plate and silverware and stepped away from the dining table, but Takao gave her a dry look.

'What? Done already? We need to talk sometimes. Dinner time is family time,' he said.

'I have a ton of homework today.'

In the kitchen, Shino washed the dishes, then loaded them into the countertop dryer. Yumi, having finished preparing her husband's dinner, was putting together a plate of curry for herself.

'Yumi!' Takao boomed. 'Is Mother home yet?'

'Your mother? She arrived just a few minutes ago. I called her when dinner was ready, but she hasn't come in yet.'

'She's been out of the house every day lately. Maybe she's made some new friends?' Takao mused. 'Shino! Go and call your grandma.'

'Okay, okay,' Shino said, suppressing her annoyance, and stepped into the hall as her father had requested. She tapped lightly on the sliding door to the guest room and called out, 'Grandma, dinner!'

'Is that you, Shino? Can you step in here for a minute, dear?'

Hearing a high-spirited voice, Shino wondered what was going on. Her grandmother – who had moved into the house about two months ago – was a bit cranky and habitually wore a frown. Shino had never seen her smile. Her lips were often pursed tightly in disapproval and there was a permanent furrow to her brow. At first, Shino had thought, *Well, she's elderly, so I should do my best to be nice.* She had gone out of her way to make conversation: 'Dad gets mad if he's not first into the bath, you know,' or 'Mum buys a lot of prepared food, but sometimes it tastes even better than home-made, don't you think?' Small observations like that. She thought she might make her grandmother laugh, but the woman just looked annoyed, and said, 'You're a chatty kid, aren't you?' So Shino had given up the effort. Their exchanges were now usually kept to the bare minimum, so what was different today?

'Oh, er . . . it's okay to come in . . .?' Shino slid open the door. Peering into the room, she could hardly believe what she saw.

'Well, what do you think? How does it look?'

Her grandmother Mitsue's hair was dyed the same pink-beige hue as Yukihime, the girl from the television show they had been watching earlier.

'Huh? Gran, but what . . .?'

Mitsue was seated in front of an old-fashioned vanity table, the likes of which Shino had only seen in comics or on TV. Gazing at herself at various angles, this way and that, she said happily, 'I wasn't sure about the colour, but it makes me feel bright and carefree, you know? I got a perm, too, because my hair's become a little thin over the years. Now it's gone from flat to fluffy. Like candy floss!' The fingertips running through her hair had been transformed as well, with rhinestone-studded gel nails.

'Uh . . . what . . .' Shino scrambled to find the right words. 'Grandma, what's happened to you?'

'Oh, I just decided I didn't want to spend the rest of my life looking so shabby. It's better to take care of oneself, isn't it? What do you think, Shino?' Mitsue smiled.

Her grandmother's eyebrows, which had been unruly when she had first moved into the house, now traced a delicate arch, and a dark patch on her right cheek had disappeared. She must have had a full makeover, because her complexion, too, was so bright, she looked like a different person. Or maybe it was better to say she had actually become a different person. When Shino had run into her that morning, her grey hair was trimmed into an old-fashioned bob, and she was wearing a sagging T-shirt with frayed cuffs and collar, shuffling along, hunched over, in baggy elastic trousers. Who could have imagined?

'Well, Shino? What do you think?'

'Oh! Well, I, er . . .'

Shino took a second look at her grandmother, this time a little more carefully. Mitsue was wearing fancy make-up, and, as she herself had noted, her hair was all puffed up like candy floss. Her clothing was on the loud side – a dress featuring an embroidered hydrangea pattern over leggings. Shino could hardly believe it, but her grandmother had even got herself a pedicure!

'Well, it looks okay, I guess . . .'

To tell the truth, Shino couldn't think of anything else to say. It did look glamorous, in a way, but perhaps because Shino was unused to seeing her grandmother look anything like this, it also seemed a bit over the top. Still, Shino wasn't close enough to her grandmother to come right out and tell her it looked weird.

'It does? It really does? Oh, that's a relief. Once I had the hair done, I started wanting some new clothes to go with it. Look here – I got quite a few.' Mitsue gestured around her. She was surrounded by shopping bags. 'Kokura is a real city, full of stylish shops and stylish people. I saw a lady my own age prancing around in the highest heels you've ever seen,' Mitsue said earnestly. 'Of course, I can't do that now, you know. I still have a bolt in my leg from when I broke it five years ago, so that's out for me.'

'Grandma, Papa says to come eat your dinner and – eek!'

Yumi had poked her head in the door, presumably to summon Mitsue to dinner, and, catching sight of her, let out an involuntary squeak.

'Oh, Yumi! What do you think? I had a makeover!' Mitsue ran her hands through her cotton-candy hair, laughing.

Dumbstruck, Yumi just kept repeating 'Oh! Oh!' then spun on her heels in a panic and called out 'Papa!'

'Oh dear, I startled her, didn't I?' Mitsue cackled gleefully.

Takao, who had come running at Yumi's call, was literally floored, sinking to his knees where he stood. 'Mother, what's happened to you?' he exclaimed, a note of hysteria creeping into his voice.

'It's cute, isn't it?' Mitsue responded, looking a little proud of herself.

'You must be crazy!' Takao shouted. 'That's . . . that's . . . what is it? Some sort of costume wig for parties, or what?'

'Don't be ridiculous, dear. It's my own hair. See?' she said, taking hold of a lock of hair and pulling it taut, so he could see. The candy floss held fast, Mitsue's light pink scalp visible in glimpses beneath it.

'Is this some sort of joke?' Takao clutched at his own head in turn. 'Mother, what's got into you all of a sudden?'

Yumi spoke up, a little more hesitantly. 'Until now, you've always led a frugal life, saved every penny. You said dyeing your hair was a waste. You've never done anything like this before.'

It was common knowledge in the Nagata household that fashion held no interest for Mitsue. Frugality was her watchword, and she owned not a scrap of designer clothing. On very special days, she'd wear a simple black blazer over a fresh-pressed dress shirt, and she made do without accessories of any sort.

'Yumi, run out right now and get us some hair dye,' said Takao. 'Mother, you're going to fix that immediately.

If you go walking around the neighbourhood like that, I'll never live it down.'

At those words, Mitsue's smile quickly vanished. 'What are you saying! After all the trouble I went through to make it pretty like this? Don't be so foolish!'

'You're the fool, Mother. I don't know what you think you're doing in that frivolous get-up. What's it about? Did you hit your head or something? Yumi, I think we should have her checked out at the hospital tomorrow. Take her there for me, will you?'

'Oh! But, dear, I have work tomorrow. I'm not sure I can take off on such short notice.'

'What does your work matter? Isn't Mother's health more important?'

'It's not that simple for me,' Yumi protested. 'I can't just check out like that!'

'Both of you stop your selfish nonsense!' Mitsue said indignantly. 'I'm not sick. This was my choice!'

The three of them launched into a heated argument.

Not wanting to get caught in the crossfire, Shino stepped into the hallway and observed the fracas from a safe distance. She should probably just have gone back to her room, but she wanted to see how things would unfold.

'Mother, enough, already,' Takao said. 'You're making a spectacle of yourself. It's pathetic.'

'You don't control what I wear, you know! If I went out in public half-naked or filthy, then maybe you could talk. But I mind my hygiene, I take care of myself. Look! Even my nails are trimmed.'

'Oh no! Not your nails, too! What's happened to them?' Takao let out a pathetic moan, as if he'd seen a ghost. 'Mother, what's got into you today? If there were a sensible explanation for all this, that would be fine, but there's not, is there?'

'And what of it?' Mitsue spoke sharply. Her customary frown had returned to her face, the lines between her brows deepening even as she spoke. But then, just as quickly, her face softened. A flush spread faintly across her cheeks.

'Grandma? What's wrong?' Seeing the change in her mother-in-law, Yumi sounded a note of concern.

Mitsue wavered for a moment, and then, as if all her high spirits until then had been a lie, spoke so quietly they could hardly hear her: 'It's just . . .' She trailed off.

Takao cupped his hand by his ear. 'Eh? Eh? What was that?'

'It's just that . . . I'm in love.'

Then it was again Takao's turn to shout, louder than anyone else had done all day.

Takao, furious, had tried to interrogate Mitsue, but she had adamantly refused to provide details on anything, most of all regarding the object of her affection. She'd just kept repeating that she'd fallen for someone, and wanted to look her best. Takao, who was taking pills for his blood pressure, had turned red in the face and nearly fainted, while Yumi, in a panic, had called a halt to the madness. But when Mitsue came in the next morning and Takao caught sight of her candy-floss hair, he almost fainted again.

'Ugh. I was hoping that was just a bad dream! Mother, what's going on? Really – are you sure you aren't sick or something? I hate to say it, but could this be an early sign of dementia?'

'Don't treat me like a fool! I'm still as sharp as ever. My life is good. I've even fallen in love.'

Shino watched the argument from the sidelines, eating

the leftover curry from the day before. When she was just about done, she said to Takao, 'Dad, you're going to be late for work.'

'Oh no! Already? Mother, I'm begging you – please put your hair back the way it was by the time I get home tonight. Okay? I've got enough problems as it is.'

Takao hurriedly pulled himself together and left the house, and in short order they could hear the growl of the car engine starting in the garage.

'Shino dear, look here, at my hair. I set it myself this morning. I think it looks pretty good!'

Mitsue seemed unbothered by her son's anger. As if she were a different person, she smiled happily and nattered on, talking about how difficult it was to add body to the area around the crown of her head.

'Wow, Grandma, you really did it,' said Shino. It was no different from yesterday, when her grandmother had come back from the salon.

'I did, didn't I?' A shy smile crept across Mitsue's face.

'So you're going to keep that hair?'

The two of them turned. Yumi, who probably should have been preparing to go to her part-time job about now, was standing there, looking annoyed.

'This is a problem. It puts Papa in a sour mood.'

'I don't know anything about that. And anyway, why should I have to tiptoe around here, just because Takao gets cranky?'

'Well, that may be true. But it also makes trouble for me.' Yumi sighed. When Takao was in a bad mood, he took it out on his wife and daughter. But the lion's share of the abuse went to Yumi.

Mitsue glared at Yumi sullenly. 'It makes no matter what I do – no need for you to worry about it one way or the other. And let's get one thing straight: it wasn't my idea to come and live here, you know. The two of you begged me to come for your own convenience, and now you're trying to put me under lock and key! Just who do you think you are?'

'I think we're family, that's who we are,' Yumi said wearily, 'and I think it would be nice if we tried to accommodate each other just a little bit.'

Mitsue had moved in about two months before, when Takao's company had downsized and he was laid off. Takao had been a section manager, so he had assumed that he'd be secure, but that had turned out to be wishful thinking. Luckily, he was able to find a placement at another company in the same field, but only at a fraction of his former salary. Their stylish Scandinavian-style home had been built in anticipation of a promotion, but now it was putting a strain on the family finances. Takao's mother had been living alone in Saga since her husband had passed away, so Takao, worried about what was to come, had asked her to sell her house and farmland, so they could use the money to pay off the mortgage on his own house. When she was told that her son and his family would be out on the streets otherwise, Mitsue had no choice but to sell off everything and move to Kitakyūshū.

'I had friends there,' Mitsue said plaintively. 'I lived there for decades. You asked me to leave my home, the one I knew so well, and now you won't even let me think of myself once in a while?'

'About that, well, yes. I really do feel sorry.' Reluctantly, Yumi bowed her head. She had loved their new home more than anyone. Although Takao had the final word in most matters, she had loudly declared that there was absolutely no way they were letting go of the house. 'But, you were getting older, you know, and I think we'd all have ended up living together sooner or later anyway. If we were in a small apartment at that point, you would have been in a real bind, right? Anyway, it would have been nice if you had mentioned the makeover to us in advance, even just a word or two. So we could be mentally prepared.'

'I can make arrangements to go to an old-age home any time, without anyone's help! And if I had asked you about the makeover first, would you or Takao have told me to do what I like? Clearly not!'

Mitsue raised her voice, to which Yumi responded, 'There are limits!' and looked sharply away. 'To be that garish at your age, well, it's just an embarrassment. What will the neighbours think of us?'

'And when you can't manage your finances responsibly at your age, what will they think of that?' Mitsue snapped back.

'Oh! You know that's not my fault. Takao told me not to bother my head about money when we got married, so talk to him about that. Do you think I enjoy having a part-time job just to balance the budget? I'm working hard enough as his wife! And besides, if he acts like a tyrant around the house, isn't that his mother's responsibility? Nobody seems to want to play the domineering husband these days except for your son.'

Watching all this, Shino stood up without saying a word. At times like these, the best thing was usually to head to school as quickly as possible.

But school right now was no fun at all.

★

When Shino arrived at her classroom, Daisuke and Yukari were standing in the hallway. They were plastered together, arms encircling each other's waists. Shino slipped past them into the classroom, working hard to resist the impulse to whack them on their heads and shout, 'Get a room!' She took her customary seat by the window, and before even saying hello, her friends Minato and Riko said in chorus, 'They're at it again this morning!'

'It's been two weeks since they got together, hasn't it? Every morning's the same. Honestly, I wish they'd give us a break. Shouldn't they be arrested for public indecency by now?'

'I mean, is she in heat? Do you think Kanazawa switched to an older girl because he thought she'd let him do it? Like maybe they've already done it.'

The two of them were smirking as they spoke, so Shino offered them a wan smile in return.

'Well, who knows, right?'

She was dying to add a few choice words of her own, despite herself. Admittedly, her feelings about the whole thing had cooled, but still, couldn't they show her a little consideration? Everyone in school knew that she had been dumped, and she felt prying eyes on her from all sides, watching to see if she showed her wounds. But any action she took would simply lower her to their level, so she was stuck. She certainly didn't want anyone to think she was jealous or anything like that.

'No, actually, they're awful. I mean, the lowest of the low. They're like monkeys. Like sex monkeys.'

'Yukari is always with one boy or another. And she's not all that cute, so they're definitely just after her body.'

Watching Minato and Riko snicker under their breath, Shino felt a kind of repugnance. *If you were only saying it for my sake*, she thought, *I'd be happy.* But that's not how it was at all. They were just dragging her into some prying, twisted game of feelings. Didn't they realise they were doing the exact same thing to her that Daisuke was doing?

Shino was on the verge of yelling at the two of them, but couldn't quite bring herself to do so. Instead, she adopted a pained tone and said, 'Ugh, I'm sorry. I've been feeling bad all morning. I keep thinking I'm going to be sick. I'd better go home.'

'What, for real? It's the two of them, isn't it?'

'Yes, it's because of those lovebirds, isn't it? Poor you . . .'

As the two of them started up in tandem, Shino fixed a smile on her face and said, 'No way, nothing like that. I'm just really feeling sick. Ever since that food poisoning, my stomach has been off. I heard bad shellfish could be awful, but it's really true.'

'Shellfish? Really? You're sure? And you're okay about Kanazawa?' Minato looked somehow disappointed. Riko, too, muttered a short 'Hmph' to herself.

'Anyway, sorry. Tell the teacher I left, okay?' Without waiting for a reply, Shino turned and left. On her way out of the room, she noticed Daisuke out of the corner of her eye – he looked puzzled to see her leave just as she had arrived – but she quickly passed him by.

Making her way against the steady stream of students entering the building, Shino was surprised at herself. This was the first time she had ever left school early because of a bad mood. Even if she was slightly out of sorts, it had never occurred to her not to go.

She thought briefly that maybe she should turn back, but as she got farther from school, the guilt quickly lightened. Instead, she began to think, *Well, I didn't really have much of a choice.* At the moment, spending any amount of time at home or at school meant a guaranteed dose of stress.

Going home meant the possibility of running into Mitsue, with her abruptly changed personality. It just felt so strange to see the woman who had worn a perpetual frown on her sour face now calling her by name with a radiant smile. Takao seemed to suspect her grandmother was sick somehow, but was there really a disease that could give a person such a cheerful disposition?

Shino didn't want to go home, and she didn't want to go back to school. She walked as far as the park near her house, then reversed course and headed back towards a convenience store that was closer to school. Shino wandered aimlessly for a while before realising she was standing in front of Moji Station.

'Hm, maybe I should go somewhere?' she mumbled. Should she take a train to Kokura? There was lots to do there. She could go and hang out in a café, or visit the city library. She could while away the whole day there.

It was a solid plan, but instead Shino boarded a train in the opposite direction, heading one stop out to the end of the line at Mojikō Harbour. Rush hour and the school commute were both well over, so there was hardly anyone on the train, and it was quiet and calm inside the car. Shino sat in a window seat and gazed at the view outside. The sea stretched out in all directions through the train window, sparkling as it bathed in the near-summer sunlight. She could see a tanker slowly making its way across the horizon. *I wish I could go far away like that*, Shino thought, but all too soon the train had glided into its final stop at the elegant early twentieth-century train station in Mojikō.

MEET ME AT THE CONVENIENCE STORE BY THE SEA

It had been a while since Shino had been to Mojikō Station. She thought the last time was probably in middle school, when she had come with her family to have a dinner of *fugu* – blowfish – a local speciality. She knew the area was a classic tourist location for Kitakyūshū, but as a local resident it was hard for her to think of it as particularly new or exciting. When she had been seeing Daisuke or when she was out with friends, the place to go was pretty much always the area around Kokura Station.

Gazing idly at a Starbucks outlet in the train station that had been done up in suitable period style, she quickly decided it was time to go outside. As she exited, the iconic plaza fountain shot up with perfect timing.

'Oh, it's so pretty!' Shino had no idea that it could do that. She watched the rhythmic changes in the motion of the water until the fountain had gone through a full cycle, then turned to her left and walked off towards the seaside.

It was a weekday, but still a few tourist types could be seen scattered here and there. People were taking photos of the train station and the men who pulled the rickshaws, standing there waiting for customers.

'Hmm . . .'

There was a young couple. The woman was wearing a resort-style sundress, and hanging tightly on to her partner's arm. Watching the two of them talking quietly to each other, oblivious to their public surroundings, a shadow fell across Shino's heart. She pretended not to see them and strode rapidly off towards the shoreline.

The promenade along the coast was elegantly paved with red brick. The broad white span of Kanmon Bridge shone brightly in the full sunlight, linking Kitakyūshū to Shimonoseki on the mainland. The clear blue of the sky and sea, the white clouds that seemed to be awaiting summer, and the vivid greens of new growth in the surrounding trees and parks were dazzling.

Somehow, Shino had never taken the time to really look at the scenery here before. She stood still for a moment, then heard an announcement coming from somewhere: 'The drawbridge is being raised.'

She scanned the area.

'Ah.'

In the distance, she could see the two sides of the bridge slowly lifting.

'There it is. The lover's whatchamacallit.'

It was the 'Blue Wing Moji', one of the largest drawbridges in Japan. It opened and closed a few times every day to let ships in and out of the harbour. There was an old story that the first couple to cross the bridge each time it came down would be bound together for life, so it was also known as 'The Lovers' Haven'. Shino remembered Daisuke inviting her to cross, when they had first started dating. *Let's make a run for it the second it touches down*, he had said, but, embarrassed, Shino had refused. If she had agreed back then, would things be different now?

At the foot of the open bridge, a few people were taking photographs. Among them were the couple Shino had noticed earlier. The young man was saying, 'I'll carry you!' to the young woman. She was wearing stiletto heels at least three inches high.

Shino veered off again, this time heading towards Kaikyo Plaza, which looked out on the scenic Kanmon Straits. It was at the heart of the area known as the Mojikō Retro District and was lined with souvenir shops, eateries and all sorts of other stores. On holidays, the plaza was flooded with tourists, and often featured on local television shows.

Looking at the arrays of speciality sweets arranged in the storefronts, the unfamiliar landscape, the tourists floating along in their own worlds, Shino felt as if she were walking through an unknown, faraway land, even though she was practically right in her own backyard. It was an unexpected feeling, different from everyday life. She felt like she, too, was floating, and her stride lightened.

In front of the locally famous 'banana man' statues – a pair of men dressed in yellow and black banana costumes, one in sunglasses, the other looking a little more serious – a couple holding a small child asked Shino if she would take their photo. The parents were all smiles, but the child kept looking at the banana men with a curious expression on her face.

Shino took a few shots with their phone and made small talk with them. Then, out of the corner of her eye, she caught a glimpse of something that looked almost like candy floss.

'Huh?' she exclaimed, surprised. Had she just seen her grandmother's head? No way, it wasn't possible. It was too far a walk from their home in Moji, and what would her grandmother want in Mojikō anyway? Did she want to see the local sights? Not likely. For the longest time after moving here, she couldn't even be bothered to take a walk around their own neighbourhood.

'Is everything okay?' asked one of the parents.

'Oh. Yes, I'm fine. Well, I should go.'

Shino bobbed her head at the couple with the child and moved away.

I must have been mistaken, Shino thought.

She shook her head and pulled out her phone. 'I guess I may as well see the sights here myself.'

She had come almost by accident and hadn't thought there was much to see, but now that she was here, part of her was a little excited.

Shino looked at a map of the area on her phone. One nice thing about Mojikō was that a lot of the sights were within walking distance. Stately buildings were scattered throughout the neighbourhood, and they were full of history and beauty. The furniture and accessories on display, too, were also spectacular. Shino had gone through a period when she had been obsessed with *Taishō Romance* video games, and one of the rooms she saw could have been pulled straight out of the world of those games, leaving her enchanted in spite of herself.

The twinge of guilt she had felt about skipping school completely evaporated. Her spirit lightened, and she thought to herself, *I really needed a reset, didn't I?*

'Hm, what to do next? There's the Idemitsu Museum of Arts. Should I go there?'

Perched lightly on the guardrail separating the promenade from the traffic, she did a quick search on her phone. All she had was her allowance, so she couldn't do anything fancy.

Just then, she noticed a comment on social media: 'The Tenderness there is wild!' Tenderness? Did they mean the convenience store? Confused, she tried to swipe back to the comment, but for some reason all it said was 'Deleted.'

'Huh?'

Shino didn't understand. Was she seeing things? There was the weird apparition of her grandmother's hair earlier, then this disappearing message – had she stepped into some sort of fairy tale?

She poked around a little more on social media, then, with a start, said, 'What am I doing?'

Even though she was just exploring with no particular destination in mind, she was wasting her time.

'Oh – but I'm hungry.'

Somehow it was already after two in the afternoon. Amazed at how the time had slipped by while she was walking, Shino took a look around. She'd pick up some rice balls and tea at a convenience store and find a good place to eat.

She walked along, keeping an eye out for a suitable store, and eventually, in the distance, a sign appeared: 'Tenderness'. Remembering the ghost post from before, she thought, *Well, I guess this must be the place*, and turned into the car park. She couldn't believe what she saw there.

The Tenderness was on the ground floor of an apartment building. Across a walkway next to it were a laundry and an empty storefront. It looked like there might be some shops on the second floor as well, but from the third floor up, the building seemed to be residential. It seemed entirely unremarkable – except that in front of the shop was a male employee – or at least she assumed that he was, based on his uniform – surrounded by a cluster of older women. For some reason, the man was holding a bouquet of bright red roses.

'This is too much. How can I accept such a lovely bouquet?' The man, who had strangely refined features, ran the fingers of one hand through his soft hair. He had long, well-proportioned limbs that matched his height well, but his face was delicate. Shino wondered if he might be a movie star.

The city of Kitakyūshū was a frequent shooting location for films and TV dramas, and Shino herself had once tried out for a role as a movie extra. It had been a golden opportunity to catch a glimpse of a popular male idol, but perhaps for that reason the competition was fierce, and she never heard back. A classmate who did get the green light, however, came back starstruck, going on and on about how all the actors were radiant and practically superhuman, and the man in the car park seemed like a perfect match for all the girl's platitudes.

Could she have wandered onto a movie set? Shino looked hastily around, but there was nobody else there.

Looking back dubiously at the group, she could see the old ladies chattering at the shop guy about something.

'Goodness, those roses certainly suit you! Not every man can pull that off. Mitsu, you're quite the charmer! Just how many of our hearts are you planning to steal today?'

'We'll give him everything, won't we? We don't care!' a granny with vivid purple hair called out to another older woman on the far side of the circle.

The woman, red-faced and nodding vigorously, was none other than Mitsue.

'Grandma?!'

Shino was so shocked, she called out without thinking. Why would her grandmother be at a convenience store in Mojikō?

'Eh? Wh-what? Shino?!' Mitsue's eyes opened wide as she turned to Shino, and she started to sputter. 'Er, ah . . . but what are you doing here? Shouldn't you be at school?' Her grandmother was obviously flustered.

Shino felt a sudden surge of panic. She wasn't ready to admit that she had skipped for the day, so she lied. 'They had a staff meeting today. They let us out early.'

'Oh! Are you Mitsue's granddaughter?' The purple-haired lady turned to Shino with a delighted smile. 'I'm

Mrs Yamai. I live here in the Golden Villa apartments. We've become quite good friends with your grandmother lately. Isn't that right?'

She looked to the others in the group for confirmation, and they all nodded. They were about the same age as Shino's grandmother, it seemed, and were similarly dressed in stylish clothing, with hair and nails carefully done up to match.

'Ah, you're with Mitsue? Nice to meet you. I'm Mitsuhiko Shiba. I manage the Tenderness store at the Golden Villa apartments here in Mojikō.' The man holding the roses gave her a broad smile.

Wow. Shino took a step back. It felt like an invisible force was emanating from his face. According to her movie-extra classmate, the actors on the shoot had an aura like that, so powerful she felt she'd get burned if she got too close. Shino had assumed she was exaggerating, since they were only human, after all. But maybe it was true? After all, the man in front of her was clearly having some kind of effect on her.

And it wasn't just Shino. The ladies closest to the man were giggling, eyes nearly crinkled shut with glee. They wore the kind of smiles that pop up involuntarily on the faces of people who are eating something extraordinarily delicious, or looking at a newborn baby.

'Mitsu dear, you're doing that thing again. You need to keep a little more distance between you and the youngster. And watch that smile, or she's going to run away!'

'That's right. Remember the other day, when the young lady fled the shop and forgot to pay?'

The ladies all laughed merrily, and one of them said to Shino, 'It's a strange thing, I know, but he really is the store manager here.'

'That man puts his whole heart into customer service. True, it's a little exciting. But that's just right for women like us. Our senses have dulled a bit over the years.'

'Once upon a time, even a wedding toast would set my head spinning, but now a glass of cold saké tastes like sugar water to me, you see?'

'Right, cold saké . . .' Shino replied vaguely, then turned to her grandmother, standing among the group of ladies and looking nervous and embarrassed in equal measures. 'Grandma, why are you here?'

'Mitsue is the newest member of our fan club,' Mrs Yamai responded before Mitsue could muster a reply.

'I was just standing there in Kaikyo Plaza one day,' said Mitsue. 'Mitsu picked me up, and it was love at first sight!'

'Er, that's not exactly . . . I had no intention . . .' Flustered, Shiba turned to Shino. 'That is, your grandmother was looking a little faint, so I spoke to her,' he said. His voice was resonant, as low and smooth as a musical instrument.

What, even his voice is dangerous? Shino thought. If one were to put it in terms of the granny who was talking about cold saké, this would have to be at the level of vodka or tequila.

'She was sitting at the side of the promenade, so I was concerned, and spoke to her. She said she lived some distance from there, so I invited her to come and rest at the dine-in space of our shop. Isn't that right?' Shiba said.

The other women laughed and nodded in agreement.

Mitsue spoke: 'I wanted to get to know my new neighbourhood, so I took a walk, but I suppose I overdid it.' She looked away, slightly shame-faced. 'Mr Shiba and the Golden Villa Ladies Association were so kind to me. It made me happy. Oh, I wish I could live here, I thought.'

'What are you saying?' Mrs Yamai stroked Mitsue's back.

The woman in the elegant sundress added, 'We're always happy to add another member to the club!'

'Every day, there's something new to look forward to. Take a look at the flowers our Mitsu is holding. They were a gift from your grandmother.'

'Yes, when I said I wanted to get the ladies something to thank them for helping me, they all said I should make it something nice for Mr Shiba.' Mitsue curled herself up even further. 'I thought for such a beautiful person, it should be roses. But I don't know much about this sort of thing. I've never really given anyone a gift like this, or received one, so I wasn't sure what was right.'

As her grandmother spoke in a small, embarrassed voice, Shino took a close look at her. Was this person standing before her really Mitsue? What had happened to the stone-faced, humourless woman she thought she knew?

'They're delightful,' Shiba said. 'I'm told that roses suit me, so to receive a beautiful bouquet like this makes my heart tremble.'

The ladies replied in chorus. 'Yes, they do suit you! And this way, we all get to enjoy a share of the beauty!'

'Ah, good point. In that case, I hope I'm not overstepping my bounds with your gift, but . . .' Shiba plucked a single rose from the bouquet and with a gentle flourish held it out to Mitsue. 'I don't want to keep something so beautiful all to myself. Let's show them off together, shall we? How about it?' Shiba said with a smile, and with a squeak of surprise, Mitsue timidly stretched out her hand to accept the rose. 'I'll put some in my room, and some in the shop,' he continued. 'Thank you for a wonderful gift, Mitsue.'

Shiba then handed a rose to Mrs Yamai, and another to the woman in the sundress. They blushed.

'Oh, Mi-chan, you're such a lovely man.'

'You've given me a new lease on life!'

'Shino – you too, please.' Finally, Shiba offered a rose to Shino.

'Um, well . . . thanks,' she mumbled, and took it. Somehow, the bright rose seemed to become just a little bit duller in her hand. Could there be a man who was so much like a rose that a rose would glow like that, just because he was the one holding it? The image of a video-game prince popped into her mind.

Shino took a quick look at the storefront behind Shiba. It didn't appear significantly different from the Tenderness store near her own home. Even though it seemed like the real thing, she couldn't help wondering if perhaps there was also a chain of Tenderness ladies' clubs.

Just then, another employee, a man whose head was shaved like a priest, leaned out from the shop doorway. Unlike the manager, he was a completely ordinary-looking man. He sported an ultra-grumpy scowl that seemed utterly wrong for a customer service job.

'Boss!' he called out. His voice seemed ordinary as well. 'Can you get back to work? It's time for my break!'

'Whoops! Sorry, Hirose, I lost track of the time.' Shiba bowed his head hurriedly and said, 'Well, duty calls. Mitsue, thank you very much for today's gift, but please know it's not at all necessary – I'm always happy just to see every-one's smiling faces.'

Breathing out the words in one smooth, sweet breath, Shiba hustled back into the store, clasping the remainder of the roses in his arms.

'Of course, Mitsu, dear! Wonderful to see you as always!' Mrs Yamai said with feeling, then turning to the group, she added, 'Shall we all go up to my place today? We have to get these roses into a vase soon, don't we? And, young lady, why don't you join us? Someone gave me a box of sweetcakes – you know, the local ones, shaped like blowfish. You'll have to help us eat them.'

Shino was swept along with the group, up to a room on the fifth floor of the building, above the convenience store.

From the conversation between the ladies, Shino learned a thing or two. First, the building was called the Golden Villa and specialised in apartments for seniors. Second, Mitsuhiko Shiba, the manager of the store, had his own fan club. The members of the club were primarily building residents, plus the occasional outsider. And lastly, that her grandmother had recently joined the club.

'A fan club?' Shino asked, taken aback.

'That's right. Mostly, we just keep things in order at the convenience store for Mitsu. We make sure the dine-in space and the parking area are neat and clean, and we keep an eye on the neighbourhood as well. Because sometimes no-good scoundrels come around to bother our Mitsu. Your grandmother said she wanted to help, so we invited her to join the club.'

'Mitsue, you said you had no friends since you moved here? I'm certain that's why Mitsu brought us all together. You'll find no shortage of friends here!'

The merry group burst out laughing, Mitsue included, albeit somewhat shyly.

'And your group is the reason for all my grandmother's changes?' Shino couldn't help but ask. There were a variety of different ladies in the group, but they all took obvious care over their looks. Everyone's hair gleamed, and it was easy to see that they had neglected neither hands nor feet in their attentions. The lady in the sundress had ornate golden filigree patterns traced on her nails, while another was wearing a sweet lily perfume. Something in her grandmother had been awakened by these women, Shino thought.

'Well, who can say? In any case, we're lucky to know her,' was all they said. 'But, certainly, our Mitsu is the best, without a doubt. Whatever we do, he's guaranteed to notice and make a kind remark. It's a joy to feel truly seen by someone who shares in your pleasure over even the very smallest things.'

'It's a blessing to have someone give you a compliment, isn't it? Especially at this age. It makes each and every day that much brighter. Doesn't it, Mitsue?'

As the flow of conversation turned her way, Mitsue nodded. 'Yes, it does.'

'You know, I was really surprised the first time someone said they liked the shape of my nails,' said one of the women. 'But then, one day, I tried polishing them, and when I heard they looked even better, I said to myself, *Next time why don't I try something even more special?*'

'Hm,' Shino murmured softly to herself. She had thought that the change in her grandmother had happened all at once yesterday, but maybe she was wrong. When she tried to remember her grandmother's appearance or behaviour, even from the past few days, she drew a complete blank. She didn't know she had been doing her nails and so forth. She didn't know she had been travelling all the way here to Mojikō.

'She was so gloomy at first that we were sure she was sick, or something like that. But you brightened up quickly, didn't you? And we're glad for that. Because it's lonely when you don't know anyone.'

'Sure, and it's rough being in an unfamiliar place. When Mrs Ōtsuka and her husband first moved here from Nagoya, he was awfully down in the dumps, wasn't he?'

'Oh, Takiji? And now he thinks about nothing but fishing, doesn't he?'

The conversation quickly shifted to other topics and Shino nibbled on her cake, forgotten. She felt as if a cold draught were whistling through her very core.

Her grandmother had been having a rough time too, Shino thought. Hadn't she said as much that very morning? That she had abandoned her home of all those decades, the place where her friends lived. Her son's family were the only ones she knew here, and had that family shown her any sympathy? Neither Shino's father nor mother, nor Shino herself, had given a thought to her grandmother's loneliness or suffering. They asked perfunctory questions like *Are you okay?* and *Are you settling in?* but nobody really gave it any serious thought. Even though she had been forced to endure a huge inconvenience for the convenience of the rest of them. They had turned a blind eye to the profound changes in her life.

Shino watched Mitsue smiling and chatting with the other ladies in the group. She spoke softly, and she seemed in every way the essence of a sweet, tender grandmother. The candy-floss hair and bright clothes that looked out of character yesterday suddenly seemed to suit her perfectly.

Shino finally realised that what she had considered the brusque, unsmiling demeanour of her grandmother was just the façade of a woman who had been unable to open her heart to a near-stranger. That kind of sharing didn't happen automatically, even between relatives.

When she thought about it, Shino had only really seen Mitsue once each year for most of her life. Takao wasn't the type to go home with any regularity, and when the family did have free time, Yumi always wanted to go to Shimonoseki, in the opposite direction, to visit her own parents. Shino saw her maternal grandparents often, and so they were very close. But her father's mother, whom they had only ever rarely seen, seemed distant and unapproachable. It felt as if she were always scrutinising Shino's every word and deed, and it made her feel inadequate.

Perhaps her grandmother also felt unequal to the task of dealing with the grandchild she saw so rarely. Perhaps she felt the same about her son and his daughter-in-law, who hardly ever visited. And yet, when they came to her weeping and begging for help, she said nothing, left her old life behind and came with them . . .

Shino bit her lip hard. She suddenly felt like a terrible person. She had dismissed her grandmother's earlier conduct as the unpleasant behaviour of a cranky old woman, and observed the furore over her recent changes as if it was a spectator sport. It was no different from how her classmates had treated her when she was dumped. They had all simply enjoyed the show, looking down from above without kindness or care, while someone's feelings were being shredded. She had felt this pain herself, and still remained indifferent to someone so close suffering through a similar situation.

Shino took a covert glance at her grandmother. As Mitsue chatted with the other ladies in the group, her eyes would occasionally light on the roses in the vase. Sometimes she'd give a gentle smile.

I've never really given anyone a gift like this, or received one, so I wasn't sure what was right.

Shino recalled the words that Mitsue had squeezed out earlier. Everyone said that her late grandfather had been full of bluster. His son had inherited this trait, which was why he was so high-handed at home. When she was a child and didn't know any better, Shino had believed with certainty that her father was a great man. But as she grew older, an uneasiness crept in, and when on a visit to her mother's parents, she overheard Yumi complaining, 'He's just a wage-earner. He's useless around the house,' she understood somehow that it wasn't high praise.

On Takao's birthday, Yumi would make him an elaborate meal and, together with Shino, present him with a gift. But Takao had never done anything comparable on Yumi's birthday. 'I got you the house you wanted, didn't I?' That was his favourite saying. And even Takao would say, 'I'm a sweetheart compared to the old man.'

Shino looked at her grandmother's face. *I wonder if she was ever truly happy*, she thought. *The way Daisuke broke up with me really hurt me. I may not love him anymore, but that doesn't make what he did all right.* There were certain kinds of respect that every living person deserved.

Shino's problems had only lasted about two weeks. But what about her grandmother? Had she been struggling her entire life . . .?

Quietly nibbling on her sweetcake, Shino had a lot to think over.

As evening was falling, Shino and Mitsue took their leave from Mrs Yamai's house.

'Shall we get an ice cream or something at the Tenderness?' Mitsue said.

Shino asked, 'Is that so we can say goodnight to the store manager?'

Mitsue's cheeks coloured slightly.

'Well . . . yes.'

In her hand, Mitsue held the two roses. Mrs Yamai had wrapped them for her. She had cut two small pieces of floral foam and soaked them in water, so the flowers would keep until she got home.

In the store, they picked out a bottle of tea and some chocolate biscuits. Shiba was at the till, and when he turned to the two of them, Shino felt inundated by the same invisible aura as before. *Whoa*, she thought, and again she recoiled involuntarily, but this time, Mitsue also took a step back. *Right, cold saké*, thought Shino, remembering. *Grandma's a lightweight.*

'Are you headed home?'

'Yes, that's right. But I'll come back again tomorrow,' Mitsue replied in a higher than usual voice.

'Of course, please do,' said Shiba. 'Everyone will be happy to see you. You too, Shino. Please come again.'

If I were older, I wonder if I'd sigh like Grandma did, Shino thought. *No way. I'm not into that kind of weirdness. I'm probably a lightweight too.*

'Okay, maybe . . .' she replied vaguely, lost in her thoughts.

Just then, a voice came from behind: 'Shino?'

She turned. It was Azusa Higaki, a classmate of hers. In her hands were a café au lait éclair and a coffee jelly parfait. They were the hottest items at the Tenderness and had been all over social media lately. Apparently, the Tenderness chain had got into a new collab with some old-school coffee store, and now people were coming to Kyushu from all over, just to purchase the stuff.

'Oh, hi, Azusa.'

'Hi, Shino! Your house isn't near here, is it?'

Azusa was a mild-mannered girl with a slightly chubby face. She and Shino sat near each other at school, so they had talked to each other a bit, and the two of them got along pretty well. From what she had heard, Azusa knew a lot about desserts and had recently developed an obsession with baking.

'No, not really close, but . . .'

'Ah. So you and Azusa are friends?' Shiba joined the conversation.

Azusa replied, 'We're in the same class.'

Shino felt slightly more at ease, and lowered her guard. She wondered if Azusa had fallen victim to the shopkeeper's mysterious aura. Or did she not notice? Anyway, it was kind of amazing that the two of them knew each other.

'Goodness, you're one of Shino's friends? Nice to meet you, I'm her grandmother.'

'Nice to meet you, too!'

After exchanging greetings with Mitsue, Azusa leaned in towards Shino and lowered her voice.

'Are you okay?'

'Huh?'

'Um, this may be none of my business, but it seems like you've been having a hard time lately.' Azusa's expression of kind concern deepened. 'This morning, you went home right after arriving at school, didn't you? I was worried that something had happened,' she added.

'Oh, that. Well . . .' For some reason, Shino felt like she could talk about it directly. Maybe because she could see the real concern in Azusa's eyes. 'Honestly, Higaki, I didn't think you noticed.'

Everyone in class knew that Shino and Daisuke had split up. Also that he'd dumped her for an older, second-year girl. But she didn't think there was a single person there who had noticed how rotten she had been feeling. She had kept her cool, and hadn't cried or made any kind of scene at school. She had made a conscious effort to act the same as always. Despite Minato and Riko's efforts to the contrary.

'It must have been really hard,' said Azusa. 'I thought it was amazing how you handled things. Holding it together the way you did, that's not easy. I know that.'

In an instant, tears were running down Shino's face.

With a start, Shiba and Mitsue both looked over in concern. 'What's wrong?'

Azusa, still holding her sweets in one hand, said, 'Oh, I'm so sorry! Sorry to spring that on you!'

'What's wrong, Shino? Is it your stomach?' Mitsue looked her in the eye, but Shino just shook her head.

'It's nothing, not like that. No, I was just, well, actually . . . I was just a little happy.'

That was it. Shino was happy.

She swiped the tears away roughly with the back of her hand.

Mitsue handed her a handkerchief. 'Here now, wipe.'

Shino took it and held it to her face. The smell was pleasant and somehow familiar. It reminded her of her grandmother's house in Saga, she realised. The old farmhouse had a sunlit veranda, and Shino suddenly recalled dozing there on summer afternoons. The warmth of the sun, the fragrance of greenery borne upon the breeze. She had slept well amid the scent of earth and flowers. It was that smell.

As she wiped away the tears, she felt a hand touch her arm. It was Azusa, who smiled hesitantly, and said, 'Shino, let's have something sweet. There's a dine-in space next door. Let's eat there. And we can talk. Okay?'

Shino looked at Azusa with eyes still wet from the tears. *Why is this girl being so nice to me?* she wondered.

The dine-in space was pleasant, tidy and devoid of other customers. Shino had imagined a narrow, confined area, and was surprised to see how large it was. There were five tall seats at a long counter, looking out through the window, and two four-seater tables with regular seats. On each of these, a vase was set, holding a single rose. Free of tears, Shino considered the space. For a convenience store, it was really pretty, she thought. It had the ambience of a chic café.

'Let's sit here.'

Azusa sat at one of the four-seat tables as if she were well used to it, and placed the sought-after café au lait éclair in front of Shino and Mitsue, who sat across from her. Mitsue had purchased three bottles of juice and set one in front of each of them.

'Sorry about that,' said Shino, still wiping her face with the handkerchief, and Azusa laughed.

'Don't worry about it! I'm the one who's sorry, for springing that on you. When I find someone interesting I always want to talk to them.' Azusa lifted her bottle gratefully, removed the cap, took a sip of the sweet drink and said, 'I've been wondering when we would have a chance to sit down together. So I'm glad we ran into each other. The truth is, I'm really drawn to people who can stand up and look you right in the eye. Because it makes me feel stronger. Like I can do it, too!'

'Um, but I'm not that cool, really.' Shino took up her own bottle. She had cursed Daisuke any number of times, but silently, to herself, and she had even imagined giving a sharp yank to Yukari's ponytail.

'Okay, well, nobody's perfect. We're all just trying our best, right?' Azusa said diplomatically.

Oh, that's true, Shino thought. *Maybe I just wanted someone to recognise how hard I was trying. Maybe I just wanted someone to care.*

'Now, Shino, tell me. What happened to you?' Mitsue looked at her intently. 'Were you bullied at school? If that's what happened, we'll go to the school and lodge a complaint.'

There was a new firmness to her voice, neither the curt tone of earlier days, nor the recent softness.

'Don't you worry about a thing. When Takao was little, he was teased, too, but your Granny was tough. I chased away those bullies with a broom!'

'What? Dad was bullied?' Despite herself, Shino let out a little snort.

'He was! That boy was a real homebody,' Mitsue said. 'Now he's a big man, but back then he was a scrawny thing, and the larger boys roughed him up something fierce. Even now, he's only strong at home. Your mother and I get to watch him storm around the house, but he won't make a squeak at work.'

'Really?' At last, a smile crept across Shino's face.

'Now then, what happened?' Mitsue asked again.

Shino wasn't sure what to say. What would her grandmother say if Shino told her she was dating a boy? She knew what her parents would do. Takao would make a big stink about it and shout, 'You're just a child! You're too young for all that!' and Yumi would scold her: 'No more dating! It upsets your father.' That was for sure. If she admitted that she had been dumped, it would be: 'Romance between kids is just a momentary thing, anyway,' or 'It's a good thing you split up before you did something that couldn't be undone.'

'Shino, you can say what you like.' Mitsue spoke gently. 'Grandma's on your side.'

'You're on my side?' Shino hadn't expected that.

'Of course I am,' said her grandmother. 'You're my one and only granddaughter. I'm on your side against anyone, even Takao.' Mitsue pushed out her chest like a warrior, and Shino's uncertainty melted away in a flood of emotion.

Mitsue heard Shino's story through, shaking her head lightly now and again as her granddaughter spoke, then she responded.

'Ah, now I see. He was cruel, that young man. When two people part, no matter who or how, dignity is important. He's young, so that may still be hard for him to grasp. Maybe someday he'll realise the way he handled things wasn't right. But it was sad for you, wasn't it, Shino?' Mitsue sighed. 'Still, you know . . .' Her voice brightened. 'It's a good thing to love someone. It's a very good thing.' Mitsue seemed to be offering these words to herself as much as to Shino. 'No matter how old you are, it's good to love someone. And when that happens, it's good to love not just the other, but also the person you yourself become through your love. Care for the other, and care for yourself equally well. Find a love like that, a love that makes you try to be worthy of the one you hold dear, and that's a blessing indeed.'

Her voice was soft and full. Listening to her, Shino thought her grandma had found an incredible kind of love. That store manager had given her the feeling that she could love even herself.

So, Shino thought, *a really incredible love can come to you at any age, and can make you happy no matter how old you are. I wonder if I'll find a healing love like that someday.*

Shino felt just a twinge of envy. Then she realised something. Even though it was pretty weird to be jealous of her grandmother's love, it was also pretty cool to have a grandmother who had found a love that even her granddaughter could envy.

'But, despite all that, you're an impressive young woman, Shino. You know that, right?' Mitsue ran her highly decorated fingernails gently through Shino's hair. 'You were treated poorly, but you stood firm, didn't you? We all have to protect what's important to us, always. People sometimes lose sight of this. Some let people walk all over them and think there's nothing to be done about it. I was like that. I was foolish enough to allow myself to be treated poorly. I thought it was selfish to protect what I cared about, that a good wife wouldn't do that. And now I'm sorry I felt that way. But, Shino, young as you are, you knew what was important. And that's impressive, isn't it?'

The concern in her voice and the comfort of her touch moved Shino to tears once again. First a single drop fell, then another. Wiping them away, she felt the pain of her first lost love slowly transform, along with the unhappy thoughts that had been eating at her heart.

'Here, Shino. Taste this.' Azusa held out the paper bag containing the éclair. 'When we taste something sweet, the heart gets just a little bit fuller. Even more so when we share with others. Right?' She smiled at Shino, who smiled back awkwardly.

I want to be someone like that, she thought. *Someone who can be there to console you during hard times, who will sit by your side while your wounds are healing.*

Shino opened the bag, and the aroma of coffee drifted up. Inside the delicate choux pastry shell, coffee-flavoured jelly sat atop beautiful layers of coffee custard and pure white whipped cream. The pastry itself was glazed with a generous layer of rich mocha icing.

'Wow. That looks so good,' she blurted out.

'Doesn't it!' replied Azusa proudly. 'It's the broken-up jelly that does the work here. When it mixes with the cream, it becomes café au lait. And the coffee custard makes the perfect bridge between the jelly and the whipped cream. The choux pastry has a nice bite to it, and the chocolate and coffee flavours in the mocha bring balance. Still, it's not too sweet, so you can eat the whole thing without feeling bad. The Tenderness sweets have been awesome this year!'

'My, you're an interesting child, aren't you?' said Mitsue.

Looking a little abashed, Azusa lapsed briefly into silence.

'Sorry, I'm really obsessed with sweets. I can get a little carried away.'

'I love talking about dreams and passions.' Mitsue bit into her share of the éclair. 'My goodness!' she said. 'That is delicious. One can find such delicious treats these days!'

The three of them devoured their éclairs happily. Before she knew it, Shino found herself smiling brightly.

Afterwards, they said goodbye to Azusa, and Shino and Mitsue headed for home, walking side by side on their way to Mojikō Station.

'Oh dear! Did you skip school?'

'Yeah. I don't know, it was just too hard to stay there. But I think I can handle it tomorrow. Azusa will be there.'

'See you tomorrow!' Azusa had said to Shino. She had smiled and said she wanted to talk more. Shino had smiled back and nodded. Knowing that Azusa would be there, Shino could go to school tomorrow.

'Grandma, are you going to tell the school?'

'You mean that my granddaughter got dumped? They'd think I was overprotective.'

Shino giggled. 'I'll be okay,' she said. And, actually, she was fine. Whatever happened with Daisuke from here on didn't matter. She might even forget about him completely. It was more important to focus on people who would look after her, not the ones who put her down for no good reason. 'Grandma? It feels good to know there's someone looking out for you. Someone who worries about you and is rooting for you. Doesn't it? When Azusa said what she said, I finally understood. So I know why you're so crazy about Mr Shiba.'

It must have been lonely for her grandmother, coming by herself to a place she didn't know, to live with a family that showed no interest in her. It wasn't about gratitude, honour or respect. What was missing was simply kindness, a show of concern from her own family. And that's surely why Mitsue had seemed so hard-nosed.

'If I tell Dad, he's going to get all ticked off, so I'll pretend I don't know, but, Grandma, I'm really glad you're going to Golden Villa and joining that fan club. I like that place. And I like those people.'

Mitsue stopped on the spot. Shino stopped too.

'What's wrong?' she asked. Now it was Mitsue who looked like she was about to cry.

'I'm just happy, Shino. You understand.' She choked up a little as she spoke. 'That's all I need. I'm glad I came here. Ah, life – you really can make a new beginning any time, can't you? I never thought the day would come when I could wear such fine clothes and spend such lively days with people. I never imagined that I'd be able to speak with my granddaughter about love and such. Oh, I'm so lucky, don't you see?'

'Aw, c'mon. It's not such a big deal.' Shino laughed off her grandmother's words, but secretly she was glad to hear them. From here on out, she didn't think she would feel so empty or lonely. 'Hey, Grandma!' she said. 'Your hair looks cute that way. Really.'

'It does, doesn't it?' her grandmother said, swelling with pride.

When they got home, Takao was already there. Apparently someone from school had informed him that Shino had left early.

'You! You skipped school? What have you been up to?' He gave Shino a rap on the head as he spoke. 'We tried to call, but you didn't answer. What is this nonsense? How could you cause your parents so much worry?'

Shino caught a sharp whiff of alcohol. *No, he's not worried at all*, she thought. He was yelling at her about missing school before he had even heard her explanation. Also, if he were worried, would he hit her like that? Plus, there he was, having his evening cocktail, just like any other day.

'Dad, why don't you try to be a little nicer to your own family?' Shino looked him in the eye as she spoke.

Her father frowned. 'What did you just say?'

'We all tiptoe around all day worrying about putting you in a bad mood. Kind of strange for a family, don't you think?'

'What's that? You talk like that to your father?'

Takao raised his hand, as if to strike her again, but quickly Mitsue stepped between the two of them. 'Shino did the right thing. She said she was sick and then came home. Once she was feeling better, I took her out for a walk with me.'

'What's that you say?'

'The girl had some troubles. I listened to them. And I was there as her guardian, so she did nothing wrong. It was wrong of me not to contact you, but, Takao, you must stop hitting your daughter when you should be talking to her instead.'

Mitsue spoke quietly but firmly.

'Huh?' Takao grunted. 'You call yourself her guardian? At your age, and with that ridiculous hair? Please, enough is enough! And you've been wandering around town like that? It's a nightmare! Yumi!'

In response to Takao's shouting, Yumi came out and handed over a plastic bag. With a truly exhausted look, she turned to Shino and Mitsue. 'Is it fun for you two, making extra trouble for me?'

'Here, Mother. Hair dye.' Takao pulled a package of dye out of the bag, for natural grey hair. He must have sent Yumi out to buy it.

Before Takao could hand over the package, it was swept aside. Not by Mitsue, but by Shino.

'I think her hair's fine the way it is!' she said to her surprised father. 'It suits her, you know. It's stylish, and cute, too. I'd be fine if Grandma came to school like this. In fact, I'd be proud. I'd brag about it. *Seventy-eight years old and she hasn't lost her sense of style*, I'd say. That's how much I like it!'

'You watch your mouth when you're speaking to your parents!'

'All right, that's enough,' her mother interjected. 'Shino, apologise to your father.'

Takao and Yumi both raised their voices and Shino fell silent. She felt guilty, particularly when her mother said she was making trouble for her. Time and again, Shino had done something thinking it was for the best, or just because she really wanted to, and had earned Takao's wrath, which he took out on Yumi.

'That applies to you too, young man! You watch your mouth when you're speaking to your mother!' Mitsue addressed Takao, then gave a quick squeeze to Shino's hand. Shino understood the meaning of that fleeting touch.

She looked up at her grandmother. Was that . . . could it be . . .? It was. It was a struggle, but Mitsue was doing her best to wink. Shino could barely contain herself – she almost started to laugh.

Chapter 2
Tarō Hirose Has the Blues

Tarō Hirose was in an exceptionally bad mood today. Annoyances were piling up, one after another.

First, six different women had given him their contact information while he was at work. Along with the contacts came a perfume-drenched calling card (just holding it was enough to contaminate his fingertips), a sexy selfie, a thick envelope stuffed with he could only imagine what, and that was just for starters.

'You be sure he gets it!'

'This has nothing to do with you, so don't get the wrong idea, understand?'

'Don't give me that look. You're not the one I'm after.'

All six of them had spoken to him as if he were nobody, without even a pretence of civility. Of course, Tarō wasn't the object of their attention. It was Mitsuhiko Shiba, the manager of the Tenderness convenience store at the Golden

Villa apartments in Mojikō, where Tarō worked part-time. But Shiba had been away for three days, summoned to the head office and temporarily assigned to another branch in the Tenderness chain, so, with no other recourse, the women had reluctantly handed over their communiqués to Tarō.

'I don't have to put up with this! Who do they think they are?'

After the women had gone, Tarō vented his frustration to Muraoka, who shared his shift. Admittedly, Tarō wasn't the most cheerful of employees, but he was always perfectly polite with customers, as one would expect from an employee at the store. So why did he have to listen to the kind of nonsense that made him question his own humanity?

'Maybe we should make a special mailbox for Mr Shiba?' Muraoka said with an earnest look. DIY projects were a special talent of his, and besides, Tarō wasn't the only one fed up with receiving gifts meant for Shiba-san.

'If you do, make it for him and his sister both,' said Tarō.

Another reason for his bad mood was that he had also been accosted by three men:

'You steer clear of Miss Jewel!'

'If you lay a hand on her, I'll have something to say about it, you hear me?'

'Yeah, stay away from her!'

Bearing a cake box, a fancy designer shopping bag and a bouquet of tulips, the men had one by one handed him their gifts, along with a few choice parting words.

Their target was Shiba's younger sister, Jewel. After graduating from high school near her home in Miyazaki prefecture, she had moved to the Golden Villa apartments in Mojikō, where her brother lived. She was working as a clerk in an insurance office on the second floor of the building while she tried to figure out what she wanted to do with herself. She would occasionally visit her brother's store to purchase this or that, and it seemed that she had acquired a following of her own.

It had been two months now since Jewel had moved into the building, and there had been a noticeable increase in the number of regular male customers, perhaps in the hopes of meeting her during one of her occasional visits to the shop. Sales had increased, which was, of course, desirable, but the staff's feelings about it were mixed. They were already besieged by her brother's fans, and now with a constantly increasing number of Jewel's suitors added to the mix, it was becoming nearly unbearable.

'Why are they threatening me, anyway?' Tarō asked.

'Because she likes you, right?'

Muraoka spoke as if it were obvious, to which Tarō snapped, 'How should I know?'

It wasn't like he had tried to charm her – he hadn't even been particularly nice to her. He had treated her very normally, he felt, the same way he tended to all customers.

But it was also true that Jewel did like him.

When Jewel saw Tarō, she'd come running like a puppy, a wide, innocent smile floating on her face – he could practically imagine her wagging her tail.

'I made too many *ohagi* dumplings – here, I brought you some.'

'We should have lunch together sometime.'

'When is your shift over? See you soon!'

Jewel was three years younger than Tarō. She was drop-dead gorgeous, with the extraordinary good looks and perfect figure of a teen idol. Nobody Tarō had ever met even came close to her. And it didn't feel bad at all to have a girl like that smile at you. But considering the reactions of her entourage, he couldn't exactly say he was glad about it, either. Because the attention of a girl that beautiful also drew hostility – plenty of it.

'I didn't do a thing to get her to like me! As if I would.' He snorted in derision, then added quietly, 'She's out of my league, anyway.'

Tarō saw himself as a very average guy, perhaps even a little below-average. Height, build, looks – nothing about him stood out. The only thing that was maybe even a little unusual about him was that he had been shaving his head since high school, but that was nothing to brag about – certainly not stylish or cool. And he had one big strike against him, which was that he had no great hopes or dreams for his future.

After graduating from university, Tarō was supposed to join his family's plumbing business. People who didn't know any better would act like that was a great thing, telling him, 'You're going to run the whole show someday.' But, actually, it was a small business very rooted in the local community. His parents ran the company together, wearing their blue work uniforms every day, and his mother's major pastime was tending to their savings.

In truth, Tarō could have started work straight after high school, but his grades were good enough for university, and his father, who had only made it as far as high school and had a bit of a complex about it, had said, 'Why don't you give it a whirl? You're still a spring chicken. Do it for me.' So Tarō had stayed in school.

Tarō's parents and grandparents had each in their turn inherited the company founded by his great-grandfather. They had worked hard to keep their customers, and he was the next in line. He understood that there was nothing wrong with that. And that some people might even envy him. But Tarō's future held neither excitement nor ambition for him. When he listened to his friends talk about their own plans, he felt a little jealous.

'Honestly, I don't know what the hell she even sees in me.'

Personally, Tarō didn't view himself as much of a catch. So Jewel's behaviour made no sense to him.

Listening to him muttering to himself, Muraoka finally broke in: 'Maybe it's just because you don't fawn all over her, Hirose. It happens all the time in manga, doesn't it? The princess gets bored with all the hangers-on and falls for some jerk who won't give her the time of day.'

'I'm not like that at all! If I acted that way, Takagi would kill me.'

Takagi was a part-time employee, two years older than Tarō. In terms of actual work experience at the store, Tarō was the senior, but he treated the older Takagi with respect. Possibly the seniority system had been burned into him by his devotion to baseball throughout his high-school years.

'Takagi, huh? Everyone knows he's her number-one fan. He doesn't keep it a secret.'

Muraoka gave a wry smile. Jewel had made her first appearance in Mojikō last Christmas, and Takagi had been instantly smitten. It was much more than a simple date that he wanted – according to Takagi, she was his dream girl, the love of his life. 'I want to be there to clear every little pebble from her path,' he had said, starry-eyed.

'Have you seen his face when she asks me out and I say no? He can't stand the idea of a guy like me spending time with her, but thinking about how rude it would be for a guy like me to turn her down makes him furious. He gets so torn apart that he just stands there looking blank.'

Tarō went deadpan in imitation, and Muraoka howled with laughter.

'Okay, but if you're not sweet on her, and you're not tough on her, then where do you stand?' Muraoka gave Tarō a long, questioning look. 'I mean, you could say you're just being polite, or interested, but that's kind of weak, isn't it?'

'Yeah, that's true, I guess.'

'So maybe we should just say you're soulmates, and leave it at that?'

'I'm not anyone's mate! Got it?'

A gentle melody rang out, announcing a customer, and Tarō turned towards the door: 'Welcome, how may I help you?'

There stood Jewel herself, beaming from ear to ear. She must have finished at work, because she was dressed casually in jeans and a T-shirt, and when their eyes met, she gave Tarō a little wave.

'Ooh, Hirose, I'm getting a little jealous,' said Muraoka. 'If someone smiled at me like that, I don't know if my heart could take it!'

In actuality, Muraoka had just taken up with a new girl. She was a former basketball player, super fit with the slim figure of a model and nearly the same height as Muraoka himself. She was nothing like Jewel, so Muraoka was clearly just kidding around.

When he received only silence in reply, he shrugged and said, 'I don't get you at all, Hirose. You don't have a girlfriend, do you? I'd think you'd be flying high right now.'

'To fly, you need wings.'

'You don't have 'em?'

'Nope.'

As Jewel ran up to him, Tarō turned to her, as always, and said, 'Welcome to the store, how may I help you?'

After work, Tarō rode home to his apartment in Shimonoseki on a Honda Hornet 250 motorcycle that he had bought with the money he earned at the Tenderness. Tarō had wanted it ever since high school, when he saw a former student he admired riding one. A sizeable portion of his salary each payday was devoted to improvements and customisations on the bike. It didn't get great mileage, and maybe it wasn't the best value, maintenance-wise, but he loved it.

Once he exited the Kanmon Tunnel, he was on Japan's main island, Honshu. It was hardly worth noting, but sometimes a map of Japan would pop into his head. He'd imagine that Honshu and Kyushu, so cleanly separated, were reaching out to touch each other, and he was a tiny bean lodged in the brief space between their outstretched fingertips.

'It's a whole wide world,' he said quietly to himself, for no particular reason.

He parked the bike at a supermarket near his apartment to pick up a few ingredients for dinner. People were often surprised to hear that Tarō liked to cook. When he'd lived alone during his first year in university, he had made the discovery and had since developed a broad repertoire of dishes.

He removed his helmet and was running through the contents of the refrigerator in his head when he heard a familiar saccharine voice.

'Tarō, sweetheart!'

Apprehensively, Tarō turned. The girl addressing him wore a tight dress that emphasised her cleavage. Her close-cropped hair highlighted large brown eyes and delicate ears, her full lips gleaming as if slicked with oil.

'Tsubaki.'

'It can't be you! It's been forever, hasn't it? Imagine running into you at a place like this!' Tsubaki laughed, shaking her head. She was arm in arm with a tall man, his hair long on top and shaved close around the sides, like a pop star.

The man, who was good-looking enough in his own way, turned to Tsubaki and asked, 'You know him?'

There was something familiar about the guy. Maybe he was a student at Shimonoseki City University, where Tarō was enrolled.

'He's a childhood friend of mine. We're just pals,' Tsubaki said carelessly. 'We've known each other since kindergarten.'

The man's eyes travelled back and forth between the two of them. He gave a tight-lipped smile. 'That so? Well then, nice to meet you.'

The man nodded at Tarō, who replied, 'Likewise,' and nodded back.

Of all the girls to run into it had to be her, he thought.

'Are you still living in that apartment, Tarō? The water pressure in the shower there was terrible.'

As Tsubaki spoke, the man she was with stiffened noticeably.

Here we go again, Tarō thought. He gave a quiet sigh.

'Whatever,' he said. 'Well, see you around . . .'

He walked away, but behind him he could hear the two of them talking as he left.

'How do you know about that guy's shower?'

'Oh – er, well, you know, I think I went there with my dad. Did I say our parents were friends?'

'Okay, I guess . . . But you wouldn't have gone for any other reason?'

Tarō pretended not to hear.

If you're going to play it like that, just come out and admit that I'm your ex-boyfriend! Screaming silently at her in his head, Tarō stepped into the supermarket.

Tsubaki and Tarō had been together from the winter of their second year in high school to the summer after his first year in university. Tarō was on his high-school baseball team, and Tsubaki was one of their supporters. At first, he had no idea that she liked him, but eventually she began to actively pursue him, and with such fervour that he was drawn to her eagerness.

Tarō's baseball team was not strong – they never made it past the regional qualifiers – but for some reason a lot of the players happened to be really good-looking, and consequently the team had become immensely popular back at school. This meant that even Tarō, with his average looks, was sought after by all the girls, just because he was a regular.

Looking back now, Tarō could see what a small world it was that contained the hierarchy he and his teammates had ruled, and how little he had understood of that back then. At the time, he was even foolish enough to think that he was a better man for it.

Tsubaki's grades weren't on a par with Tarō's, but she didn't want to be apart from him, so when he'd enrolled at Shimonoseki City University, she'd followed him there and found work at a nail salon in the city.

Those were happy days, or so it seemed.

Tarō tossed some bean sprouts into the basket he was holding. There was some leftover pork at home, so he thought he'd do a simple vegetable stir-fry to go with it, but while he shopped, he continued to think about days gone by.

They had basically been living together at that point, free from their parents' prying eyes. Tsubaki seemed to have it rough at her new job for about a month, it must have been, but after that she grew more polished with each passing day. Her black hair became a trendy shade of brown, her eyelashes grew longer, and her eyes seemed to be a different colour every time he looked. She turned to attention-grabbing clothes as well, showcasing the lines of her relatively ample figure. Back in high school, she had been the demure type, not even wearing make-up, but soon she was transforming into an adult woman right before his eyes.

Tarō could only watch in wonder at Tsubaki's changes. He had friends who had come out of their shells in university, but that was nothing compared to Tsubaki. *Women are amazing*, he marvelled.

Sometimes Tsubaki would say to him, 'Say, Tarō, why don't you try to mix things up, too?' But Tarō couldn't get into the idea and just stuck with things as they had always been. It wasn't a question of principle – he had just lacked the will to change. Now he wondered if his reluctance was only because he had been so popular in high school just as he was.

Tarō thought that Tsubaki had stopped wanting to go out with him about the same time, more or less, as when their feelings about things like this diverged, but a chorus of friends agreed that things had gone south long before that. By the time Tsubaki had started tending to her looks, she was already two-timing Tarō.

'You've lost the spark you had in high school,' Tsubaki had told him sadly, when they split. 'Oh, but it's not your fault. You know that, right? I just didn't have enough experience – I mean, I knew nothing about the world, did I? I finally realised that there were so many people in the world who had that spark. Like you did, Tarō, or even more than you. I mean, it's like if you only knew the light of fireflies and then discovered that there was fire in the world, and electricity. Wouldn't you want to experience all those new, shinier things?'

It had been a warm summer day, the cicadas buzzing extra loud. They were standing by the entrance to their apartment building, and Tsubaki was wearing an airy slip dress. Her neck had glowed as if it was now releasing all the sunlight it had collected during the day. Tarō had looked at her, sweat running down his temples.

Tsubaki had learned how big the world was during the months right after they had graduated from high school, but for Tarō that same period ushered in the realisation that he had been nothing more than a big fish in a small pond. There were so many more students in university, and so many different kinds of people, that Tarō simply got lost in the crowd.

Well, I guess there was really nothing special about me, was there?

He had never been a particularly strong baseball player, so once he reached university, that was out. Nor was he particularly talented when it came to his studies. His looks were ordinary, and he didn't have the speaking skills to draw any attention that way. Actually, he had to admit that there was nothing likeable about him at all. He felt like he had no choice but to recognise that his former popularity was unfounded, but Tsubaki had really put the final nail in the coffin.

'If I don't have a spark anymore, that's not my fault,' Tarō had retorted, feeling whatever pride he had been carrying unawares crumble into tiny pieces. 'I never thought of myself that way. You only saw what you wanted to see.'

Tsubaki had frowned. 'That's an ugly way to put it,' she'd said. 'Okay, Tarō. Well, this is goodbye.' She had sounded condescending, somehow. When he saw the cold look on her face, Tarō knew it was over. The mysterious spell that held them together had been broken. Like Cinderella after midnight, there was nothing he could do or say. He wouldn't hear her innocent laughter as she called his name anymore. Because when you looked at him objectively, there was nothing remotely interesting about him.

Green peppers were on special offer. Tarō put a bag of them into his basket, along with some cucumbers and two blocks of tofu that were also marked down, then he let out a heavy sigh.

The latest thing at the Tenderness was the Plus Alpha series. These were semi-home-made dishes that the customer could easily 'heat and complete' by adding a few ingredients of their own.

'This one is really good,' said one of the regular customers to Tarō, holding up a packet for Málà Tofu. You just mixed the sauce with some crumbled tofu, zapped it in the microwave and it was done, just like that.

The customer was a man they called the 'Whatever Guy'. Tarō didn't know his actual name, although one of the veterans on staff, Mitsuri Nakao, would sometimes address him as 'Tsugi'.

'These sorts of things never have enough meat in them. Even if the main focus is tofu, you want to taste the meat, right? This one is off the hook – just exploding with meaty flavour. And then, if you mix it with the tempura set over there, it's crazy good. Especially the aubergine – it's the best. I guess that makes sense. *Mapo* aubergine is a classic, right?'

To Tarō, the Whatever Guy was just another customer. Shiba and Nakao seemed more familiar with him, but he wasn't sure how they had met him or what the relationship there was.

Still, Tarō was a little curious. The man was cloaked in a mysterious aura, and it wasn't just his unkempt hair, bristly beard or the light green jumpsuit he wore as regularly as a uniform. There were also his beautiful eyes that peered out occasionally from gaps in his shaggy hair, his clean, white teeth, his strong, balanced physique, his gruff but never violent manner – it showed through in myriad ways, Tarō thought.

Honestly, if you cleaned him up a little, he'd be handsome.

Although Tarō was reluctant to admit it, Shiba was probably the best-looking guy he knew. But he couldn't help thinking that with a little beard trim and a trip to the hairstylist, this Whatever Guy might even surpass him.

But, all that aside, Tarō wasn't sure why the Whatever Guy was talking to him in the first place.

'Er . . . Málà Tofu, you said?'

Tarō wasn't quite sure how to respond appropriately, but it wasn't the first time that a customer had started a conversation with him, so he figured he could handle it.

He cast a cursory glance at the prepared foods shelf and, quickly looking over the items, said, 'Cellophane noodles.'

'Hm?' said the Whatever Guy, looking interested.

'You might like to try mixing it with the Chinese cellophane noodle salad.'

The man's eyes lit up. 'Oh! That sounds like it could hit the spot.'

'Málà noodles salad is pretty good.'

'You've got taste, I can tell.'

The Whatever Guy was in the process of checking out, but he dashed over to grab a packet of the noodle salad, then came galloping back to the till.

'I'll take it,' he said simply.

Tarō said, 'Right, thank you very much,' and scanned the package.

The man paid for it, then dropped it in the shopping bag along with his other items.

'So then . . . Hirose?'

Holding his shopping bag, the Whatever Guy suddenly addressed Tarō by name. Tarō was startled for a second, then realised it was written on his name tag.

'Yes, how may I help you?'

Inwardly, he braced himself. What was this about? When he thought about it, there was a time when he had harboured suspicions about his manager and the Whatever Guy. Was it something to do with Shiba? The manager was in the shop today, but he was currently on his break and had retired to his apartment upstairs. Tarō couldn't tell all that to a customer.

'Well, you see, I was thinking . . . how about we grab a bite to eat together sometime after work?' The Whatever Guy sounded a little embarrassed.

Tarō's mouth gaped in surprise. 'What?'

Who, me? He's got to be kidding.

Tarō stood there, dumbstruck, until the Whatever Guy added confidentially, 'Well, actually, that is, it's about Jewel.'
Jewel? Tarō thought. *I don't believe it. This guy's after her too?* Tarō didn't know his exact age, but he was clearly over thirty – and he was chasing after a recent high-school graduate? Tarō knew age didn't necessarily matter when it came to love, but still . . . And anyway, there was nothing between Tarō and Jewel. Why was this guy asking him about her?

In the midst of his confusion, the melody announcing a new customer rang out, and an angry voice shouted, 'Hey, you there!'

Tarō swivelled in the direction of the doors and saw a vaguely familiar-looking man enter the shop.

'Is there a Hirose working here? Oh it's you, isn't it, you little bald-headed shit?'

The man laid into Tarō as soon as he recognised him.

'Welcome to the store. May I ask who's speaking?'

If there was one thing Tarō had learned in his two years working at the Tenderness, it was how to handle difficult customers coming into the shop and going off on some incomprehensible tangent. Whether it was a young man arriving to declare his love for Jewel, or a group of women in the midst of a catfight tumbling in off the street, Tarō had seen it all. Shouters didn't faze him in the slightest.

'You don't get to ask anything, understand? This is about Tsubaki!'

The man's voice got rougher, and with a start, Tarō finally realised this was the man from the other day at the supermarket.

'Oh, right. Yeah, I remember. What do you want from me? Er, didn't Tsubaki already explain that we were just friends?'

'That's a damn lie. She has a photo of the two of you, kissing!'

Not this again! I mean, this is just too much, Tsubaki. In his heart, Tarō let loose a silent scream.

'Yeah, sorry about that. But you understand that photo was from right after high school?'

Tsubaki liked to drop little hints about her past relationship with Tarō. It seemed to get worse with each new boyfriend. It started innocently enough, with comments like 'I saw that movie with Tarō,' or 'We used to go there together.' But it quickly grew more suggestive: 'That looks like the first hotel we ever stayed at,' or 'Tarō likes this underwear too.'

Naturally, if the guy was new, he'd get jealous and seek out Tarō on the university campus or at his apartment, which was near Tsubaki's place, and the shouting would begin. Each time, he'd have to explain again that Tsubaki had dumped him long ago and that they hadn't had anything to do with each other since then. Sometimes he'd even have to show them the call log on his mobile phone to prove it.

'Honestly, I haven't done anything worth worrying about. I mean, did Tsubaki put you up to this?'

In his private life, Tarō could still forgive all of this. When it happened on campus, onlookers might laugh: 'A lovers' tiff! That's too funny.' Meanwhile, his friends, who knew the backstory, would say, 'Oh no, here we go again,' and buy him a drink. But now it was happening at work.

'This is really a hassle, you know,' Tarō said calmly. 'It's rude.'

'Huh? You're the rude one, skulking in the shadows like that. Think you can put on that innocent mug while you steal my girl? Don't push your luck!'

'Please, just go home.'

There was a customer right in front of him, waiting to be served. And one of the grannies from the Golden Villa apartments was waiting at the beverage counter.

'I'm working right now. If you want to talk, then come and see me when I'm not in uniform.'

Tarō pointed towards the door, and the man coloured visibly.

'Are you making fun of me? Don't try to hide behind that till there. I came here to set you straight, you little shit.'

'Go home, you.' The Whatever Guy, who had been given a front-row seat to the proceedings, spoke in a low voice. 'Don't mess with a man's livelihood.'

The anger in the man's voice was enough to give even Tarō a start. His eyes blazed fiercely through his wild hair.

The other man took a step back. 'D-don't stick your nose . . .'

'Into other people's business?' the Whatever Guy finished. 'Then you don't bother a man while he's at work. Got it?' He took a step forward, and the other man left the store in a hurry.

Takagi, who had been restocking bottled drinks at the back of the shop, came forward, curious. 'Is something up? What's going on?'

'No, nothing worth mentioning,' said the Whatever Guy nonchalantly. 'A bug got in, and I chased it out. Isn't that right, ma'am?'

He turned to the older woman, who had witnessed the incident from start to finish, and winked. She grinned and responded, 'That's right, just a fly.' The patrons of the Tenderness were well used to such goings-on.

'Sorry about that,' said Tarō to the Whatever Guy, whose eyes were twinkling kindly as if nothing out of the ordinary had happened. 'That got out of hand. And, er . . . thank you.'

'Don't worry about it. It wasn't your fault. I thought you handled it well.' The Whatever Guy nodded a couple of times, and then leaned in close and continued in a quiet voice. 'So then, back to what we were saying. You want to get something to eat after work?'

'Me? But why?'

'Jewel said she wanted to get together with you.'

Tarō didn't understand. He stood there, just blinking.

At last, the Whatever Guy pointed at himself and said, 'I'm the big brother.'

'What? The manager is her brother.'

'I'm his big brother too.'

Tarō's brain stopped working. *Wait, wait, wait* . . . So his pheromone-drenched headache of a store manager was the shaggy guy's brother? And beautiful young Jewel was their sister?

'Oh. I forgot to introduce myself. I'm Nihiko Shiba. But everyone calls me Tsugi.'

'Ah. Er . . . really?'

Tarō was surprised, but at the same time it made a kind of sense. The three of them had one thing in common, and that was the spark. The same spark that Tarō seemed to be lacking, that drew people's attention, these siblings were just shining. You could call them the Sparkle Set. Tarō had once thought he was one of them, but it turned out that he belonged to a different tribe.

'Okay, but, well . . . why me?' he asked. 'There's no reason for her to be interested in me.'

Tsugi scratched his bearded cheek awkwardly. 'Well, we can talk about it over some good food. Anyway, I'll come by again.'

Tsugi departed, leaving Tarō puzzled about a number of things.

Just after he left, Shiba returned from his break, and the atmosphere inside the store changed markedly. Not because the manager was wearing a special scent or fragrance, but the number of customers increased noticeably, as if there were a hidden camera somewhere and they had just been waiting for him to show up.

'Hirose. Working hard as always,' Shiba said with a smile.

'Thanks, you too,' Tarō replied. Then he took a close look at Shiba's face.

'What? Is there something there?' The store manager rubbed his cheek, looking slightly flustered.

The gesture was weirdly captivating, Tarō thought, and as if to confirm this, someone called out from the books aisle: 'He's so adorable!'

'I was just having a Danish. Hirose, are there crumbs on my face?'

Shiba turned his lovely eyes querulously to Tarō, who tutted quietly in annoyance.

'I don't see a thing.'

'Always teasing me, aren't you?'

Tarō looked away from Shiba's ever so slightly concerned frown and let out a quiet sigh.

When he arrived home after work that day, Tsubaki was standing at his apartment door.

'Tarō, sweetheart!' She was all smiles, but he just grimaced in response.

'What's the deal?' he said. 'That boyfriend of yours, or whatever he is – quit telling him every little thing about me, okay? Enough is enough. I don't want him showing up at work again.'

Tsubaki's lips curled strangely. It seemed she was trying to suppress a smile.

She never used to act so unpleasantly back then, thought Tarō.

'So, it's true? He really went all the way over there . . .'

'Huh? You came here just to find that out?' Tarō was appalled.

Seemingly unaware of his dismay, Tsubaki gushed, 'I didn't think he was the type to do that! Hey, that must mean he really likes me, don't you think?'

'I have no idea! The point is, stop telling people where I work! I'm telling you, it's seriously annoying.'

He heaved a deep sigh of frustration, but Tsubaki just gave him a sideways look and asked, 'Tarō, sweetie, are you mad at me?'

'Obviously. You have a job, too, Tsubaki! Don't you get it? That's a line you don't cross.'

'It wasn't me, anyway, it was my guy who did it, all on his own.'

'Well, you didn't need to tell him anything about us. Why don't you just forget about me, already?'

In what world did the dumped partner have to talk like this to the one who dumped him? Tarō gave another deep sigh, and Tsubaki's eyes filled with tears.

'That's so cruel! Are you saying you've forgotten me?'

'What do you want from me?' She was probably hoping he'd say, 'Of course I think of you!' or 'I'll never forget you.' But if he said anything like that, Tsubaki would only use it against him. 'It's a pointless question.'

'Pointless? But, Tarō, sweetheart, you'll always be special to me . . .'

'You think I'm happy to hear that?'

Tarō found himself wanting to sigh in despair, again and again. They said that a single sigh of sadness could chase away happiness, but that didn't matter to him at all now, he thought, as long as it chased Tsubaki away along with it.

'So are you saying you want to get back together?' he asked, changing tack. 'If that's it, feel free to come in. I can get off, at least. Actually, I've been hard up lately, it would help to let off some steam.'

Tsubaki's face flushed instantly. 'That's awful! How could you be so cruel?'

'If you want to do it, come on in.'

Of course, Tarō didn't mean a word he said. As far as he was concerned, the two of them had closed the book on their relationship long ago, and he hadn't the slightest desire to get back together. Even Tsubaki's gestures and expressions that he had once found so adorable now just prompted a vague feeling of nostalgia, like looking at an old photo. Trying to rekindle the relationship with this girl that he had once liked would only make him feel empty now, he thought.

'If that's not what you want, then leave now. Go and see your boyfriend, or whatever he is.'

He pushed Tsubaki aside and opened his front door.

'I'll go, then! Anyway, I can tell you still have feelings for me.'

'Maybe for your body, but that's it. Bye.'

He closed the door and locked it behind him.

'Stupid! You're the worst!' Tsubaki shouted, pounding on the door, but without a response from Tarō, she eventually gave up and left.

As he listened to her storm off, he muttered to himself, 'I should have just told her straight out. I don't want to be the measuring stick for your love life.'

After she'd split with Tarō, Tsubaki's first official boyfriend was a stylist from the beauty salon next door to her nail salon. He was twenty-eight, and things had seemed good at first, but it turned out he was just toying with her while he lived with another woman. The other woman, a former television model, was infinitely more glamorous than even the newly improved Tsubaki and heaped abuse upon her when the truth came out: *I can't believe you cheated on me with such a pathetic excuse for a woman!*

Next was a student from Tarō's university, two years his senior. He, too, seemed to count Tsubaki as just one of his playthings.

The third worked in the kitchen of a family restaurant, and didn't fool around, but liked to gamble. When he lost, he'd take it out on Tsubaki. Verbal abuse turned to physical abuse and in the end, she fled.

There was a fourth man, and then a fifth, but Tarō couldn't shake the feeling that none of them really cared for Tsubaki at all.

'She just goes for anyone who comes on to her. She doesn't really take the time to get to know them first, so it never works out.' A former friend of Tsubaki summed it up like this, after sharing the details of Tsubaki's love life with Tarō. Apparently, Tsubaki had learned to do her make-up and changed the way she dressed, and when that earned her some attention, she just got carried away. She thought she should be able to upgrade to a higher-status man, but it wasn't going well, so she was floundering. 'Sure, she's hit another level of cuteness compared with the old days,' said the friend. 'But, you know, it's not that big a change in the grand scheme of things. Because there are always a million more beautiful women in the world, right?'

'You should tell her all of that,' Tarō had said.

'No way!' she'd responded, and laughed. 'Our friendship is dead. It ended the moment she called my boyfriend a loser.'

The boy this woman was seeing happened to be a high-school friend of Tarō's. He was in the Shogi club. Compared with the baseball team, it was a relatively modest, low-key group of chess players, but all the members were actually pretty interesting characters. Through his contact with the group, Tarō himself had got into Shogi, and made it to where he could hold his own at mid-level play online. He still had an occasional friendly game with some of the old club members, but ever since she had moved to Shimonoseki and become beautiful, Tsubaki dismissed them all as 'losers'.

'One thing I can say, Tarō – of all the boys she's dated, you're the one who cared for her the most. I think she knows that herself, on some level, but she doesn't want to admit it. I mean, imagine if the only one who ever cared for you was the one you dumped because he was too uncool! That's why she always talks about you to other guys. She wants to make them jealous. She wants to believe they love her more than you did.'

He had laughed off that story as ridiculous – when was it? During his second year in university, it must have been. Would she really use him like that? he wondered. But almost two years later, she was still dropping hints about him to every new boyfriend.

At first, he'd thought, *Whatever makes her happy*. That once she managed to meet someone decent, she'd forget about him. But Tsubaki's relationships never seemed to work out. Whether it was due to the hints she dropped about Tarō or not, they just didn't last. And if she was hooking up with any guy who came her way, as that former friend had suggested, then maybe that was only to be expected.

I should just come right out and tell her, he thought. *That if she's not happy unless she's testing her partner, then the relationship is pointless. That she should be in a relationship where she and her partner truly care for each other.*

But then, why should he have to be the one to tell her all that? Why should he show any feeling at all for a woman who continued to use him as an ego trip, even after she'd left him?

'Ugh. What should I do?'

Tarō shook his head. Whenever he and Tsubaki got into it, he always ended up feeling diminished somehow, like he was less of a man.

One evening several days later, Tarō had finished work and was going to get his motorcycle from the car park when Tsugi appeared.

'Hey there, Hirose. Work's done, now. You free?'

Tarō was surprised. 'How'd you know my shift?' he asked.

'Just a hunch,' Tsugi replied. 'And while we're on the subject, I get the feeling you have nothing lined up for tonight.'

'Amazing. You must have a sixth sense . . .' Tarō, who indeed had nothing on his schedule, spoke stiffly, but Tsugi didn't seem to notice.

'My hunches tend to hit the mark,' he said. 'I met a monk on a mountain retreat once, way back when. The guy said I had a guardian spirit with real sharp senses watching over me. A load of snake oil, if you ask me . . . but that's another subject. The important thing is, are you free for dinner? I'm going out with my brother and sister, and you should come too.'

Ugh. Honestly, Tarō didn't want to go. What was he supposed to say, face to face with those three? He grimaced.

Then Tsugi took a sudden, sharp look at Tarō's beloved motorbike. 'You know what's even more important, that's a great bike you've got there. It really gleams. You didn't miss a spot. You're taking good care of it, I can tell. How long have you had it?'

'What? Oh, about two years, I guess. I started working part-time here during my first year of university, and when I had saved up enough, I bought it.'

'You've got good taste.'

Tarō's heart leapt. For a while now, he had been happier to have compliments lavished on his bike than to receive them himself. These days, anyone who praised his bike was automatically in his good books.

Tsugi continued. 'You know, I have a biker friend or two. One rides a Hornet like you. He's really customised it, and he's getting pretty popular on YouTube. Maybe you know him?'

He mentioned a name. It was a biker Tarō worshipped. He even subscribed to the guy's channel.

'Whoa, seriously? For real? I've seen all his clips! He's from Kumamoto, right?'

'Yep, that's right. I got to know him when I was riding the Aso Panorama Line, I think – you know, the one up in the mountains with all the great views.'

Now Tarō was completely disarmed. How could a friend of such motorcycle royalty be a bad person in any way?

Before he knew it, Tarō was walking into a pub with Tsugi, and just as quickly they were happily raising their glasses to each other. Tarō's drink was half empty before he realised he hadn't arranged for a place to spend the night. He had a friend from university whose parents lived in the area. He thought about giving him a call, then wondered if it would be easier just to try to catch the last bus home.

As if he could read Tarō's thoughts, Tsugi broke in: 'You can stay at my place tonight. Bikers have dumped so many books at my place, I could open a little bookstore.'

When Tarō learned that his motorcycle idol had also stayed there, the issue was decided.

'For real? And it's okay with you? Sounds like paradise.'

His mood lifted. He was seized by an exhilaration that he only felt when he was in the presence of someone truly charismatic. It prompted a vague recollection of how he used to follow around the cool older boys that he had admired so much in high school. There was something sweetly nostalgic about it.

As Tarō chatted away happily with Tsugi, there was a sudden stir near the entrance of the pub, and looking over, he saw that Jewel and Shiba had just entered together. He noticed how easily they drew the attention of the tipsy patrons around them. People stared, looking here and there to see if there were cameras, assuming perhaps that it had to be a TV or film shoot. Their actions were quite familiar to anyone who had spent time at the Golden Villa Tenderness.

'Hey, over here!'

Tsugi waved, and Jewel's face instantly brightened. Beaming, she joined Tarō and Tsugi at the four-seat *tatami* table that they had occupied.

'Sorry I'm late. Ooh, Tsugi, you brought Hirose? You're the best! Hi, Hirose!'

Jewel kicked off her sandals as she spoke, while Shiba picked them up as if he were her devoted servant and arranged them neatly by the side of the *tatami* mat. Jewel quickly claimed the seat next to Tarō.

'When Mitsu asks, you always say no. I knew Tsugi could do it!'

'He's always a little wary of me, isn't he?' Shiba asked. 'Good to see you, Hirose. Nice work today.'

Shiba grinned, and the cramped seating area seemed brighter at once. Tarō marvelled at the power of these three siblings. The tucked-away corner of this easy-going neighbourhood pub, the sort of place he'd frequent casually with university friends, suddenly felt special, luxurious. Although, at the same time, it was a little bit stifling. Whatever it was that cloaked the three of them was so strong that it was almost overwhelming. Of course, if he actually said anything like that he'd likely be chased down by a mob of their fans.

Well, anyway, that explains it, Tarō thought. Now he knew why the manager had been asking him so often lately if he was hungry.

Recently, Shiba had in fact been inviting him out to eat. Of course, he had declined.

'There was no reason to go,' Tarō said flatly. 'I just didn't want to be yanked around after work, so I said no thanks.'

Shiba gave a hurt howl in reply. 'You're a hard one, Hirose!'

'Nothing hard about it. Putting up with you is part of the job description, but I'm not working overtime.'

'Ain't it the truth!' Tsugi howled with laughter. 'I know what you're going through.'

A waiter came, and Jewel and Shiba ordered drinks. Jewel turned to Tarō. 'Listen, I'm sorry for dragging you here.' She bowed her head. 'Mitsu said I shouldn't overdo it, but I really wanted to have a proper conversation with you, at least once, so here we are.'

'Okay . . . but why?' Tarō had come because he and Tsugi had hit it off, but apparently this was all at Jewel's request. 'There's no reason for someone like you to be interested in me.'

Why him, of all people? Compared with the Sparkle Set, he was practically invisible.

When he asked, Jewel cocked her head slightly to the side. Her beautiful hair swayed softly. 'What? But I'm totally interested in you. Because you're fascinating.' She spoke as if it were the most obvious thing in the world. 'You give Mitsu a hard time, but despite that, everyone at the Golden Villa adores you. Plus, we have so much in common, don't we?' Jewel lifted her crossbody bag and held it out to Tarō. 'Hirose, you're the only one who ever remarked upon my Magical Shigeru keychain and my Doomsday Cult charm!'

The keychain was promotional merchandise from a late-night anime that had aired about ten years earlier, and the charm was the mascot for a one-hit-wonder band from at least twice that long ago. The two objects had been attached to Jewel's bag when she first came to the shop to say hello. They were practically antiques at that point, and Tarō had been surprised to see them looking so clean and shiny-new. He had remarked upon them in spite of himself, and Jewel had laughed. 'I always thought when I got older, I'd put them on my favourite bag, so I took really good care of them. You like them?' Tarō had nodded. He had been hugely into the anime series, and his dad had liked the band, so they would listen to them together all the time.

'Yeah, but that was just a chance thing, really.'

'Not true! How many people remember all of Shigeru's power moves and can also tell you the birthday of the vocalist St. Goetz?' Jewel turned to her brothers. 'That's true, isn't it?'

After some prompting, they nodded sagely, Shiba saying, 'If you know, you know,' and Tsugi murmuring, 'The anime thing was news to me.'

'I'm sure you could find lots of people like that, if you were willing to look anywhere in Japan. There are even people who would study up on it, as long as you were the one asking,' said Tarō.

'That makes no sense at all. Besides, you know all sorts of other cool things, don't you, Hirose? Everyone says that you can connect with just about anyone. Muraoka said you talk about games with him. Takagi said you know all about musicians. Mitsuri said you even talk about customising recipes with her.' Jewel laughed in wonder. 'You know so many different things! So I wanted to talk with you myself.'

'But that's . . . I mean, not really . . .' Tarō squirmed in his seat, uncharacteristically embarrassed. It was the first time anyone had spoken to him this way.

'He's got the goods on motorbikes, too,' Tsugi said. 'Interested people are interesting, aren't they? People who know all there is to know about one thing are impressive. But people with range are cool, too. They're always tossing around great unexpected ideas, and it's exciting.'

Now, that was a real first.

From the start, Tarō had always been the type to have wide-ranging interests. But after he and Tsubaki split up, he had very deliberately tried to take a broader view of things. At the very least, he thought, the extra knowledge would lend him some confidence. He didn't want to be a shallow kind of person, so he'd tried his hand at this and that, hoping something would stick. But the only areas he had got deeply into were motorcycles and cooking, and even those weren't at a high enough level to impress anyone. He had thought of himself as something of a failure thus far, so Tsugi's words sent a jolt of happiness through him.

'Um, thanks,' said Tarō, trying to suppress a grin.

'I get it,' Shiba said. 'The point is, some people are so profound you want to dive into the depths of their world and lose yourself, while others see a world so wide you want them to sweep you away and lead you by the hand through it. They each have their charms, don't they? Personally, I want both.'

Shiba's words, delivered with their strange seductive energy, promptly extinguished Tarō's excitement. He wondered, *Why is it that everything this guy says annoys me?*

Just then, a young waiter arrived bearing their food and said, 'H-here you go . . .' in a strangled voice.

Another pointless conquest, thought Tarō, exasperated.

Tsugi thrust a beer stein at his brother, saying, 'Okay, now shut up and drink.'

Shiba looked a little dejected, but raised the glass to his mouth.

'I wanted to talk to you too,' Tsugi added. 'To see what you're made of. Not to brag, and I don't know why, but our sister has a real eye for people. If she wants to know someone, or even gets curious about them, there's usually a pretty good reason.' Tsugi drained his own mug and grinned. 'Honestly, anyone who works at that Golden Villa can't possibly be boring, right?'

'But I'm just an everyday, ordinary guy!'

It made Tarō feel a little lonely to say it. He didn't know how they had come to such a mistaken conclusion, but he knew better than anyone that he had nothing special going for him.

Did the three of them understand this at all? That even as they sat there, all eyes in the pub were fixed on them? That their beauty and radiance made them truly special?

People like that would never understand. They had never been dealt a reality check by life.

Tarō felt a sudden uncontrollable chill in his heart and, for lack of anything better to do, forced a wan smile onto his face.

'It's too easy to get lost among all the different personalities in the world. At least for a nobody like me, with no real personality of my own.'

He didn't think he had drunk too much, but somehow the words just slipped out.

Damn, he thought, *now I've done it*, as Shiba looked up.

'I don't think you're a nobody, Hirose. I think you have a very strong personality.'

'What are you talking about?'

'That's my question. What are *you* talking about? I like you – I don't want to hear you saying you're nobody! Isn't that right, Jewel?' Shiba said, and Jewel nodded. 'A word like "personality" is hard to define,' Shiba continued, 'but it has to be about the part of you that draws people's attention, right? Well then, you're somebody. I'm the one who's got no personality.'

'What? That's just—'

'For instance, imagine I could magically change how I looked right now, this very moment,' Shiba said. 'Then what? What if I could become a nobody, like you say you are? If I looked like you, do you think I'd just fade into the background? Become unnoticeable?'

Under Shiba's unwavering gaze, Tarō shot back, 'No, no chance of that.' He thought for a moment. 'Your looks aren't the reason everyone likes you. It's more like, I don't know, all the love you have. That's the key.'

Anyone could see that. Just by watching Shiba in the store. When he was face to face with a customer, Shiba radiated constant, sincere love for the person in front of him, no matter who. That kind of single-minded devotion was captivating. Of course, his physical beauty and strange, dizzying aura were also a big part of it, but they weren't the essence of the man.

Tarō had never told anyone this, and didn't plan to in the future, but Shiba's unique brand of customer service had once come to his rescue in a big way.

Once, just after Tsubaki had dumped him, when his self-confidence was totally shattered, he took a bicycle ride and ended up going all the way to Mojikō. He had been pedalling around madly in an attempt to escape the cloud of dark feelings encircling him. He felt totally worthless, a pathetic shell of a human being.

He hadn't had a real workout since he had quit baseball, so, before long, his breath ran ragged and his calves and thighs were screaming in protest. He was sweating – drenched, actually. He needed to rehydrate, so he'd ducked into a random convenience store that turned out to be the Golden Villa Tenderness.

As usual, the store was full to bursting with women, all flocking around Shiba. Puzzling over the scene, Tarō had grabbed a drink, but as he moved towards the till, there was a terrible pain in his leg, a really bad cramp. He gave a yelp and tumbled to the floor.

Shiba had darted over. 'Are you okay?' the store manager had asked, offering his hand.

When he saw his face, Tarō had thought about Tsubaki's words. *Okay, so this is what it means to have a spark.* Before such an overwhelmingly radiant presence, Tarō had a sharp feeling of inadequacy.

'Yeah, I'm fine.'

That gentle smile. Seeing himself reflected in those pretty eyes, Tarō drew a breath.

Shiba had helped him to the adjacent dine-in space and tended to him efficiently but diligently. 'You didn't hit your head, did you?' he'd asked, delicate brows knit in concern. 'Are you in any pain?' He really seemed to care.

'What? Oh . . . look, I'm really sorry about all this.' Tarō had hung his head. His collapse had caused a disruption in the store, however brief. The crowd of people around the man seemed to have entirely vanished. Just as he was kicking himself inside for making so much trouble, Shiba had smiled.

'It's a good thing it happened here,' he'd said, 'so we were able to help you right away. But you must be exhausted, riding all the way from Shimonoseki. Take your time. Rest a while here.'

'Isn't it a bother? Me being here, I mean.'

Shiba had offered him a sports drink and Tarō took it without meeting the manager's gaze. Even as he did, he'd thought, *What am I saying? I'm just drawing more attention to myself.*

'Why would it be a bother?' Shiba had seemed genuinely surprised. 'It couldn't possibly be. You're a valued customer of the store. A valued customer of mine.'

Ordinarily, Tarō would have scoffed at that. It seemed overblown. After all, he wasn't spending big money, he was just a regular convenience store customer. But, for some reason, those words lit up his heart like a sunbeam.

'You're an important customer, you are.'

Suddenly, tears had welled up in Tarō's eyes. He'd wiped them away in a hurry, thinking, *Why this, all of a sudden?*

Shiba took no notice of the tears, just said, 'You can't rest properly with me hovering over you. I'll come check on you later.' Then he'd returned to the store.

Alone in the empty dine-in space, Tarō had wept. He was happy to be important to someone. It didn't matter that it was just a few polite words from a clerk at a convenience store he'd never visited before. Just when he was feeling like he might be swallowed up and vanish into the vastness of the world, someone had come along and acknowledged his existence. That simple act felt like nothing less than a rescue to him.

If Tarō hadn't met Shiba then, he surely would have spent much more time in misery. He might be stuck still, worrying over his insubstantial existence, paralysed in the face of his own inadequacy.

Why would the man treat a customer with such care? Was that just a one-off thing? Did he sense that I was in bad shape? While he was still marvelling over that, Tarō had learned that the convenience store was hiring, and immediately applied for a job.

Once he started working at the store, Tarō was astonished to learn that this was Shiba's ordinary approach to customer care. The store manager tried to treat each and every customer that way, whether it amounted to dozens, hundreds or even thousands of people. It was crazy. Dealing with one person face to face was hard enough, let alone in numbers like that. Tarō wondered how long the manager could keep it up. Wouldn't he burn out eventually? He couldn't possibly show so much love for every customer. Nobody would ask that of a convenience store clerk.

But when it came to his customers, Shiba always led with love.

Consequently, the store's customer base kept expanding. Dealing with the resultant crowds was a hassle, Tarō thought, but one that he had to accept without complaint. After all, he had been one of the beneficiaries of all that love.

Looking at Shiba now, in the pub, Tarō answered honestly. 'I think you might lose a handful of fans if you looked like me, but the ones who saw the real you, beneath the surface, would stay for sure. So no matter what you looked like, you'd never disappear in the crowd.'

Shiba smiled. It was like a rose blossoming, like a whole garden full of buds bursting into bloom.

'Ugh,' said Tarō, wincing. He felt like someone had sprayed perfume straight up his nose. He thought he might sneeze.

'Oh come on now, what's this? What are you grinning about?'

'I'm just happy.'

Shiba dissolved into giggles.

In contrast, Tsugi said with all seriousness, 'Now you get it, don't you? The *real you* that you're talking about, that's your personality. That's what draws people's attention. We see the real you, and we think, yeah, it looks good to us.'

Tarō was startled. *The real me? Does such a thing even exist?*

'You know, you're pretty impressive. You go to university, you cook, you work — you're really taking care of yourself. It's cool, actually. The real you is solid.' Tsugi's eyes crinkled.

Ah, how does this guy always know exactly what to say? Tarō had thought Tsugi was sketchy, but he was totally cool. He deeply regretted his former doubts. He only wished he'd noticed the man's good points sooner.

'Are you buttering me up?' Tarō tried to pass it off as a joke, to conceal how deeply moved he was. 'Tsugi, if you're trying to sell me something, I'll buy it.'

Tsugi burst into hearty laughter. 'Mitsu's the one who sells stuff. I'd never stoop so low.'

'What? Hold on there, big brother. That's not fair.' Jewel broke in. 'Listen, Hirose! Why should my brothers have all the fun? I want in. Let's get back to Magic Shigeru, okay?'

The three siblings were really in their element now. Laughing together with them, Tarō felt a knot that had long been wound tightly inside him quietly release, and in its place stretched a new backbone, strong and true.

I'm okay just as I am.

The next day, Tarō was off work, so with nothing better to do, he accompanied Tsugi and Jewel to Karato Market. Karato was a busy marketplace in Shimonoseki, just across the Kanmon Straits, full of stalls and vendors selling all manner of fish and prepared foods. Jewel hadn't done much sightseeing since moving to the area and had been griping that she never got to go anywhere interesting. Tsugi, always looking for a tasty treat, had quickly seized upon the opportunity: 'Let's find some sushi!'

So Karato Market became the destination. Shiba wanted to come too, but someone had to watch the store, so he was hauled off protesting by his veteran employee Nakao, who shared his shift.

'It's a beautiful day. Let's eat outside!'

The south side of the market faced the sea and featured a broad wooden deck. There was also a neatly manicured grass lawn, and you could see the streets of Mojikō laid out across the water in the distance. As Tsugi had remarked, it was a bright and cheerful day in May without a cloud in the sky. A pleasant sea breeze played lightly over their faces.

'Ooh, it's so beautiful! So much wide-open space!' Jewel wore a smile of pure joy.

Watching her happy face, Tarō felt suddenly drawn to her. And then, just as quickly, he panicked: *What are you thinking? To fall for a girl like this just as you're getting over your own personal insecurities, that's begging for trouble. She's completely out of your league. Just calm down! Don't you have enough to deal with already?*

Jewel couldn't possibly like him in a romantic way, thought Tarō. She was just curious about him, and happened to be interested in things he knew a lot about. That seemed obvious from their conversation the previous day. If he fell for her, he'd be walking a very difficult path. To hold her attention, he'd have to be a person of real substance, and besides, she had no end of potential suitors waiting in the wings. If Takagi ever found out how he felt, he'd never forgive him. Plus, there were those intense brothers of hers, like caricatures, almost.

And, impossibly, Tarō had heard there were two more brothers. The oldest Shiba brother, Ichihiko, was a hermit who had hidden himself away on some mountain or other overseas, and the fourth brother, Shihiko, was some kind of world traveller, currently decamped somewhere in the vicinity of Egypt. From those few details alone, you could tell they were cut from the same cloth. It was crazy. What was it with the Shiba family?

'You live in such a beautiful city, Hirose. It's amazing here!' Jewel smiled at him, and Tarō's heart leapt.

No, get a grip on yourself! Be cool, he told himself. *Think about this girl's family. This is definitely more than you can handle.*

Out loud, he just said, 'Really? Well, actually, it's my first time coming here.'

Tarō had been living in Shimonoseki for four years now but had never once visited this area. Trying to settle his feelings, he scanned the surrounding scenery and his breath caught in his throat. The blue of the sea, and the blue of the sky. Cars running briskly over the bridge. Ships moving slowly through the water. It was a surprisingly heartening scene. He couldn't believe that this place had been waiting here, all along, to be discovered. He should have come to see it sooner. He'd wasted so much time, hadn't he?

'Tarō? What's the matter?' His sudden silence hadn't escaped Jewel's attention.

'Oh . . . it's nothing, really. I was just thinking that there are probably a lot of things like this. It's like I could have been so happy, so much sooner, if I had only realised they were here.'

He'd probably discover more things like that as life went on. And always regret them.

Jewel nodded. 'I know what you mean. I need to figure out what to do with myself too. I don't want to wait.' She leaned back, stretching slightly. 'Whatever I'm going to do with my life, I want to start doing it as soon as possible. I don't want to be sorry later that I held back.'

'Yeah, I get that.'

Even as he replied, Tarō remembered that he himself had no special goal in life. The years had passed him by, one after another, without him finding it – or even trying to find it – and now he was in his fourth and final year of university. When he graduated, he would follow in his parents' footsteps and work at the family business. Someone in his position shouldn't even bother to go looking for a dream. That was perhaps why all his interests in life had remained so scattered and shallow. Deep down inside, hadn't a part of him always held back, kept him from getting too involved in anything?

'You're getting it wrong.' Tsugi joined the conversation, through a mouthful of fried blowfish that he had picked up somewhere in the market. 'Frustration and impatience, detours and hold-ups – if you don't face those, you won't appreciate what you do achieve. How can you care about something you take for granted? The hard-won prize shines brightest.' He munched on another piece of fried fish, golden-brown and fragrant. 'Most treasures don't sparkle at all until you hold them in your hands,' he said. A few crumbs of the crispy batter glistened in his beard. 'You listening, Jewel? Big brother just tossed you a pearl.'

'Hmm? Tsugi, that fish looks delicious. Don't be a hog,' Jewel huffed. 'Hand it over now – all of it, please!'

'You're not listening, are you? Don't let that pearl get away. I'll buy you some fish of your own, so pipe down!'

Tarō watched the siblings squabble over the fried fish.

His worries about his own lack of self-confidence seemed to have vanished overnight. That alone seemed to knock the jumble of problems in his head into some semblance of order. The next item on the list suddenly stood in sharp relief.

I can't just lie back and let myself be carried along into the family business like this.

He had thought he was okay with it. That things were just going to be that way, and he could accept it. But there was a clear voice inside him, worrying about a future devoid of possibility, and he was beginning to feel like he couldn't ignore that voice any longer. Time was passing him by, while he limped along, resigned to his fate. He needed to grapple with the problem. If things kept on as they were, not only would he fail to appreciate all that he'd been given, but he might even come to resent it.

Maybe he should go back home, try telling his parents about the doubts he was having?

Man, what's got into me? he thought. *I hardly recognise myself.*

It was hard to believe he could really face up to the doubts that had been eating away at him all these years, confront the unhappiness from which he had always averted his gaze. Could someone change their outlook so easily? Maybe that was just how it worked. A kind glance, a casual but caring word – these things gave you a little push. A gentle force that could change people.

He looked up. High above him, a white bird drew a graceful arc across the deep blue sky.

'Hirose? You're in another world. What do you see up there?' Jewel looked at him wonderingly, and he snapped back to reality.

'Tsugi, Jewel – sorry, but I've got to go and take care of something. I'll see you soon.'

His companions stared at him.

'I just remembered there's someone I've got to talk to. I'm feeling like it can't wait, so . . . Sorry!' Tarō bobbed his head and ran. He hopped on his bike and gunned the engine.

It might be totally out of place. And, actually, who am I to be talking? But I think I need to say it anyway. For her sake, at least.

He sped along the road to her house, a road he had travelled so often long ago. Tarō soaked in the surrounding scenery, remembering the good times they had once had.

He rang the bell, and a man came out. The same one who had been in such a fury at the store the other day. He looked at Tarō, who was a little bit out of breath, and growled threateningly, 'What, you again?'

'Sorry, I just need a minute with Tsubaki . . .'

'Yeah? Tsubaki, get out here!'

The man seemed to be in a foul mood that had nothing to do with Tarō. He shouted back into the house and, presently, Tsubaki emerged, her face streaked with tears. She had a red mark on her cheek.

'What? Did he hit you?'

Tarō looked at the man in surprise, but the guy just said, 'It's her fault for cheating,' and gave her another smack on the head. 'That's three guys she's seeing, counting you! And she's nothing special. Who needs trash like her, anyway?'

The man spat out the words and stormed off, while Tsubaki sank to the floor and began to cry.

'I get anxious, that's all. I just want him to care about me. I just want him to love me . . .'

Tsubaki's frail shoulders trembled as she sobbed. She had been full-figured when she and Tarō were dating. When had she become so thin?

Tarō closed his eyes tightly for a moment, as if her fragile form were evidence of his neglect.

'You have to find someone who will care for you, Tsubaki. Really and truly care for you.'

Tsubaki had been wiping the tears from her eyes. Her hand froze.

'You should be with someone you don't have to test all the time. I understand the anxiety, I really do. I know what it's like to worry about whether you matter to someone. But I'm just as sure that someone exists who won't make you feel that way. Someone who will tell you that you're important, who will care for you, who makes you feel safe, who puts your heart at ease. I know they're out there somewhere.'

Tsubaki looked up at him, her eyes brimming once again with tears. 'But there's nobody like that, really . . . Unless . . . Tarō, are you saying the two of us should try again . . .?'

'Well, that . . . I'm sorry, no. I can't be that person for you anymore.'

His words left no room for doubt. Tsubaki's face crumpled.

Tarō continued. 'I don't feel the way I used to. The truth is, for a long time now, I've been dismissing everything you've been doing as annoying, or even stupid. I came here to own up to that.'

'What? That's awful . . .' Tsubaki's voice trembled. A tear rolled off her cheek, then another.

'That's right. It's really awful. I think so too. But that's not all. I meant what I said, but at the same time, I also need to tell you that I want you to be happy, I really do, from the bottom of my heart.'

Tarō knelt before Tsubaki and peered into her naked face, now washed clean of all cosmetics.

'I could never bring myself to tell you this, but I'll say it now. The time that we were together was a really happy time for me. I was lucky to spend it with you.'

From high school through his first summer at university, every day Tarō spent with Tsubaki was full of fun and happiness. Tarō believed he could do anything and be anything, and that was largely due to Tsubaki. She had declared her love with such passion that he thought better of himself than he deserved to think. She had even followed him to Shimonoseki. She had loved him at every turn, with every fibre of her being.

'If I ever seemed to have that spark you used to talk about, it was always thanks to you. When we split up, I said it was the only thing you cared about. But the truth is, you were always the one who lit that spark in me.'

Tarō this, Tarō that. Just hearing his name in her mouth lent him the confidence to think he was a better man.

'Tsubaki, you have the power to make even a nobody like me shine. You're a wonderful woman. So quit dating men that don't understand how great you are, who treat you like something disposable. You're too good to waste yourself that way.'

'But . . . but I . . .' Tsubaki buried her face in her hands.

Tarō reached out a hand to touch her hair, but then stopped himself.

'It's okay,' he said. 'It's been years since we split up. We can't go back to the way things used to be. I think you know that as well as I do. But I will never, ever forget you. I'll never forget how important you were to me, and how you made me shine. And that's also how I know that there's someone out there who will care for you even more than I did.'

It was hard for Tarō to find the right words. That was frustrating. Shiba would have spoken with real passion, and Tsugi would have been totally cool, but Tarō could only say it his own way, as best he could. He sent out a silent prayer as he spoke that what he was feeling would touch Tsubaki and give her strength to take the next step forward.

Without warning, Tsubaki peeled her hands from her face and, making a fist, struck Tarō lightly in the chest. Once, twice. 'So you don't like me anymore?'

'No, it's not that.'

But they couldn't see each other the way they used to. If they tried to get back together again, it wouldn't go well.

After a long silence, Tsubaki let out a sigh. 'I was a fool to leave you, Tarō.'

'Oh, I don't know . . .'

'I think you were the one to make me shine.' Tsubaki smiled, ever so slightly. She had changed her hair colour, her nails, her make-up over and over again, and each time Tarō was full of praise, telling her how cute she looked, how pretty she was. 'You were the real reason I felt so beautiful.' Her voice caught a little. It reminded Tarō of the old Tsubaki, somehow.

'You are beautiful,' he said. 'You've always been beautiful, Shigeko.'

Tsubaki flushed, startled at the use of her given name. 'You know I don't use that name anymore! That's off limits!' A fiery note crept into her voice.

Now *that* seemed more like the Tsubaki he knew. Somehow, there was something a little nostalgic about it.

Tarō Hirose was in an exceptionally bad mood today. Annoyances were piling up, one after another.

'Why? Why do Shiba and his siblings mess me around like this!'

Tarō had been busy all day dealing with utter nonsense. Chasing off a Shiba fan who was secretly filming the store, mediating a fight between two of Jewel's admirers and attending to a mysterious group that wanted to rent the dine-in space next door for some incomprehensible gathering of Shiba groupies. Tarō was handling all of it, solo.

'Where the hell is he, anyway? I'm missing my break!'

'He's outside, isn't he? With his fan club.'

At Muraoka's words, Tarō looked out the storefront window and spied Shiba, surrounded by the female residents of the Golden Villa apartments. He was struggling under the weight of a massive bouquet of roses, of all things. Tarō rolled his eyes. Why would they give him those deep red roses for no special occasion, on a random weekday afternoon? It made no sense.

Tarō ducked outside and called – yelled, rather – at Shiba. 'Boss! Can you get back to work? It's time for my break!'

Making no attempt to conceal his ill humour, Tarō headed back into the store. As he was muttering to himself about his impossible manager, a voice called his name from the dine-in space.

'Hirose! Isn't it time for your break? Want to eat with us?'

It was Jewel, smiling at him. Tsugi was with her too. Somehow, he hadn't seen them come in.

'Yeah? Sure, I'll be right over!'

As Tarō returned to the checkout counter, Muraoka gave him a knowing look and grinned.

'Hirose, did you find yourself a pair of wings, by any chance? You're positively glowing.'

Tarō raised a hand to his face, but he couldn't hide the fact that the corners of his mouth were clearly lifting into a smile.

Muraoka let out a long, appreciative whistle as Tarō responded, quietly, but clearly, 'Yeah. I guess I might have found my wings.'

Chapter Three
The Downfall of the Queen

It was best not to have anything to do with their classmate Shima Kurihara.

Or at least that was the word that reached Mizuki Murai, with the summer holiday nearly upon her.

'She's always hanging out with freaks. I'm telling you, she's bad news.' Apparently, Kurihara had been spotted after school and on weekends with the kind of people you'd never pick for friends. First, there was a shaggy man wearing a loud, brightly coloured coverall, and then a balding, old grandfather type in red overalls, riding a red bicycle. Way too much information, really, but anyway, that's how the story went.

'My friend said she also saw her with the muumuu lady. You know who I mean, don't you? The one who's always at the Cha-Cha Town mall, wearing those gaudy muumuus all summer long.'

This was all according to Erina Mito, a girl Mizuki had become friendly with when she started high school. Erina was pretty enough to draw stares, and had a boyfriend the same age at a different school. Apparently, the two of them had attended middle school together and started dating there. Erina also had two girlfriends in their class from that same middle school, both of them flashy, fashion-conscious types, and the three of them had adopted Mizuki into their group. Erina said she thought Mizuki would fit right in. Mizuki had no feelings about it in particular, but she went along with them.

'I don't know anything about the muumuu lady or any of that,' Mizuki replied curtly, without looking up from the book she was reading. Actually, she was pretty sure the old man in the overalls was Old Red, a well-known local character. He was always popping up here and there around Mojikō, riding his red cargo bike, and when he passed by, he'd shout, 'Hello, have a good day! Take care, now!' He wore a near-constant grin that, somehow, when combined with his rough features, had absolutely terrified her in primary school. But she had never heard anything really bad about the man, and a number of adults in the community actually seemed pretty friendly with him, so he was probably harmless.

Nonetheless, Mizuki didn't like him. He still scared her a little, and she couldn't figure out what he was up to, riding around like that all the time. He called himself 'Mojikō's tourist ambassador', but how could he say that, really, looking the way he did? When you thought about it, it was sort of amazing that nobody had reported him to the police.

'Kurihara, she's from Tokyo, right?' In their homeroom on the first day of school, they had all had to introduce themselves. Mizuki was pretty sure that Kurihara had said she'd moved there from Tokyo.

'That's right. She may be from Tokyo, but even so, she's a real loser.' Erina giggled, and gestured with her chin towards the far corner of the room, where Kurihara was perched in a seat by the window, scribbling intently in her notebook. The existing hunch in her back had become even more pronounced, and she leaned so far over her desk that her face almost touched it. The pink frames of her glasses sparkled in the early-summer sunlight.

Mizuki knew next to nothing about Kurihara Shima. They had been classmates for a few months now, but they probably hadn't even said so much as hello to each other. She was short and skinny, with dark black hair cropped razor-short in the back. Mizuki could picture her heavy eyebrows and pink glasses, but couldn't quite recall the details of her face.

'Well, she doesn't really have a sense of style,' Mizuki said. She looked at Kurihara's ears, which seemed pretty enough. She was the complete opposite of Erina, who took pains to look her best, at least to the extent that she could do so without violating any school rules. *Which means we probably wouldn't get along, anyway*, she thought. So far, she hadn't become friends with anyone inclined to slack off on their personal care or let their looks go. Or to cut their hair short, for that matter.

'Well, with those looks, nothing would suit her, anyway.' Erina laughed. 'She looks like a primary-school student, doesn't she? And then – have you heard her talk? She has a total cartoon voice! It's so weird, like she's speaking through her nose, and then she always adds "yeah?" to the end of every sentence, like literally "this, yeah?" or "that, yeah?"'. It's like she's imitating some anime character. It's so cringe, it's hilarious. Like, she's completely obsessed. It's just too perfect.'

Mizuki replied vaguely, 'So, she likes anime. Hm . . . Okay, but what does that have to do with her weird friends?'

'No idea. But if it's older men like that? Maybe sugar daddies? They could be paying her.' Erina spoke quietly, but a cruel edge had crept into her voice. 'I heard there are guys with Lolita fetishes, that sort of thing. A girl like her would be in hot demand with that sort.'

'No way, that can't be it.' Mizuki didn't know much about Old Red, but he seemed more the type to chase off a pervert than to be one. Besides, watching Kurihara as she scribbled in her book with her mechanical pencil, Mizuki thought that she wasn't the type either. She seemed like a child engrossed in a game.

But Erina just scowled and said, 'You can't judge a book by its cover. That sort of thing actually happens, you know? I mean, it's a problem, right? A girl like her walking around in her school uniform with people like that. Because if people start to think students at our school are okay with prostitution, then we're all in trouble. It's already easy enough for some people to get the wrong idea about girls like us.'

'Yes, well maybe . . .' There was some sense in that, Mizuki thought. If two people who were clearly not related to each other were strolling through town in a suggestive way, and one of them was wearing the school's uniform, there was no knowing what kind of misunderstandings or even trouble might come up. 'But why would she do something like that?'

'I don't know. I wish there were someone who could tell us what happened to her in middle school, but there isn't. Ami and Saori are saying they're going to tell the teacher.'

Ami and Saori were the other members of Erina's circle. Both were cute and somewhat conservative. As far as Mizuki could tell, they always followed along behind the strong-willed and outspoken Erina. If the two of them were going to the teacher, they must have been harbouring similar suspicions about Kurihara's behaviour.

'So, you think she's that dangerous?'

'A high-school girl and a dirty old man? Trouble for sure. I mean, she doesn't even have any friends, right?'

'Really?'

'I think everyone probably sees how much trouble she could be, so they avoid her. We need to be careful too. Being in the same class with someone like that is the worst. I mean, seriously.' Erina shook her head, and as she did, their teacher entered the room.

'Okay, people! Let's finish up here, and we can all be on our way home!'

Their form teacher, Satoko Hayashi, was an energetic and attractive woman in her thirties, popular with Mizuki's classmates. She stood straight and tall, and always wore a bright white blouse. Students would watch admiringly as she walked briskly through the playground, beautiful black hair tied into a swaying ponytail. Mizuki liked her, too.

With Miss Hayashi's arrival, the disordered clamour of the students as they approached the end of the school day settled quickly into silence.

Mizuki closed the book she was reading and glanced at Kurihara. She was still writing in her notebook. Mizuki noticed that the side of her hand on the page had turned black with lead from the pencil.

'All right now, Kurihara. Attention, please!'

At Miss Hayashi's admonition, Kurihara looked up with a start, then smiled. 'Sorry! I was just working on ideas for the Tenderness autumn bentō line, yeah?'

Her voice was definitely unusual, thought Mizuki. It did sound a lot like the voice of a cartoon character that she had loved as a child.

Someone in the class tittered.

'Eh?' Miss Hayashi's mouth dropped open.

'Miss Hayashi, didn't you hear?' said Kurihara. 'They started accepting submissions yesterday. They're making a line of autumn-themed bentō lunches, yeah? If they choose your idea, they'll make your bentō and sell it at their stores, and the winners receive an original Tenderness pre-paid gift card, yeah? Just imagine what they'd say if I shopped with that!'

'That's enough nonsense, now. Settle down and pay attention!' Miss Hayashi spoke unusually sharply.

The students giggled, and Erina said, 'What a freak!' in a voice loud enough that even Kurihara could hear. Watching all this, Mizuki made a firm determination not to have anything to do with the girl. If she were to engage with someone so weird, she'd be sure to regret it.

Mizuki thought back to an incident that had occurred about a year ago. During her last year in middle school, she had been drawn into something with a classmate who was acting in similarly incomprehensible ways. The girl, Nayuta Taguchi, had been disrupting the atmosphere in class, so Mizuki had tried to warn her. At the time, the mood in the classroom had been really bad. Nayuta's attendance was irregular – sometimes she'd show up for class, sometimes not, and when she did, she'd often leave just as quickly. She had cut her long hair short, too, and refused to change out of her gym clothes, which she had begun to wear all day long. And despite all that, she wouldn't explain why. It was clearly not normal, and it made everyone feel kind of anxious in a way that was hard to describe. So, on behalf of the class, Mizuki had decided to speak to her. To tell her not to disrupt the group, for everyone's sake.

If Nayuta had only shared the reasons for her odd behaviour, Mizuki wouldn't have had to treat her that way at all. She might have supported her instead. Maybe she could even have helped a little to lighten the burden of the girl's problems.

But Nayuta never said anything, she just disappeared. And somehow, by scolding her, Mizuki also lost one of her oldest childhood friends.

Mizuki had thought it was the right thing to do, so she had spoken out. Admittedly, she had spoken forcefully. But she certainly wasn't the only one responsible for that. Nayuta had a hand in it as well. It was too bad that she was going through such a hard time. But that didn't absolve her from responsibility. Why should she get a free pass on explaining herself?

In her mind's eye, she could see the faces of the two girls, Nayuta Taguchi and her oldest childhood friend, Azusa Higaki, one after the other. Unconsciously, Mizuki bit her lip.

Truth be told, Azusa was supposed to be here now, together in high school with Mizuki. It was an all-girls school, where their two mothers – lifelong best friends – had met, and cemented their own friendship. Mizuki had always dreamed that she and Azusa would be here together, as their mothers had been, and both remembered so fondly. But after the incident with Nayuta, Azusa and Mizuki drifted apart. Azusa had decided to apply to a different school, and now they rarely saw one another.

Her very best friend from childhood, whom she had looked after like a little sister for the longest time. She had understood Mizuki like nobody else ever could. And still . . .

Why, Azusa? There were times even now when she wanted to shout it out. They were supposed to wear the same uniform, take the same train to school. There were so many things they were going to do together in high school, and now none of that was possible.

It wasn't supposed to happen this way, Mizuki couldn't help thinking. *At the time, I just did what I thought was right. So why did Azusa look at me like that? Ah, if only Nayuta hadn't been such a mess in class, none of this would have happened.*

A mixture of self-pity and regret whirled within her. She had experienced this many times before, and although she always wished to escape it, she could never find a way.

Mizuki pushed away the tormenting feelings and turned her eyes towards the lectern, where Miss Hayashi was addressing the class.

After school, Mizuki had plans to meet Erina and the others. They were all going to Cha-Cha Town to see a movie with Erina's boyfriend, Atsushi Yoshikawa, and his friends. It was a love story that had been all the rage lately, but, honestly, Mizuki wasn't that into the idea. She didn't like that kind of sentimental mush, and on top of that, she had trouble concentrating on movies when she was with a large group, so it wasn't really her thing.

Yoshikawa and his friends in particular were the kind of boys who liked hanging out at the cinema more than they liked actually seeing the picture, and the last time they went they had talked non-stop throughout, which was really annoying. She had tried telling them to be quiet and watch, but they wouldn't listen to her at all. She was a little shocked when they just laughed her off. 'Don't you know how to have fun?' they said, and she had nearly responded, 'Don't you know how to enjoy a movie properly?' but instead she'd bit her tongue.

It was a waste of money. That's what Mizuki thought, but she had gone along anyway, because being in Erina's circle would make life at school easier.

Things had settled down a lot since the first few weeks, so it was harder to make a move to a new group now, and going it alone was out of the question.

'Hey, Mizuki, I heard that in middle school you were the Queen of Hearts. That right?' Her interlocutor was Sasuke Kosaka, one of Yoshikawa's friends. They were killing time at an arcade by the cinema.

'What? Don't be ridiculous!'

Mizuki laughed as she absent-mindedly watched Erina and her friends playing an arcade game, but Kosaka continued.

'The Queen of Hearts! From *Alice in Wonderland*. I heard from a guy who went to middle school with you. I guess you must have been really scary.'

'I don't get it. I was class president and so on, so maybe it was because I was in charge of things sometimes. But, I mean – the Queen of Hearts? I don't even know what that means.'

'You know. The Queen. You don't talk back to her, or else. *Off with her head!*'

Ah, so that's what he meant. Mizuki frowned, remembering the story. 'I still don't get it. It's not like I was some kind of self-absorbed dictator, you know.'

'Aw, come on,' Kosaka continued. 'You were really scary, weren't you? It was legendary. I heard stories!'

'For real?' Erina, who had exhausted her stock of coins, joined the conversation, laughing. 'In our class, Mizuki is super quiet and well-behaved. I don't see her bossing anyone around. Right, Ami?'

Erina turned to Ami, next to her, who looked a little troubled, but nodded all the same. 'Right. Mizuki's not scary. But I heard that she used to be. That she made her test-prep teacher quit his job.'

'Oh! I heard that too. Like, she got a group of kids to gang up on him, and it triggered some kind of depression?'

'What?! I didn't make him quit!' Mizuki's voice lifted a notch, involuntarily. In fact, they had all told the teacher what they thought of him, and it was true that he eventually quit. But they hadn't ganged up on him, or drove him to depression, or anything like that. 'We just thought his teaching style needed improvement, and pointed that out.'

'Really? Well, that's not what I heard. I heard you were like a queen on her throne. Like, everyone had to agree with everything you said, or if you got mad they'd be dead to the whole class. Just like that.'

'I'm telling you, it wasn't like that! That's a complete exaggeration.'

Maybe it had felt a little bit like that at times? Everyone had gone off to different high schools now, but her classmates back then tended to follow her lead. Still, that was just because she paid attention to what was proper, and knew how to do the right thing. Nobody had ever contradicted her because nobody had ever thought she was wrong.

After all, everyone who disagreed with her ended up leaving, didn't they?

'I wonder if it's true . . . Mizuki, the Queen of Hearts, beautiful but severe. Interesting, right?' Kosaka snickered, and Mizuki turned to look at him. He was a decent-enough-looking boy, except for a bad case of acne dotting his cheeks.

'Come on – it wasn't like that, okay?' She kept her tone light, but her mind was elsewhere. *I wonder if Azusa thought I acted like the Queen?*

'Hey, the movie's about to start. Let's go.' Yoshikawa checked his phone and headed off. The group followed him, with Mizuki at the rear. As they walked, she heard laughter, and looked back.

It was Kurihara, standing at the entrance gate to the Ferris wheel. An older woman in a hot pink muumuu was there too, arms and legs swinging wildly around in a sort of approximation of a dance, while Kurihara clapped along in time with the woman's moves and laughed.

'Mizuki, hurry up . . . Oh! Is that Kurihara?' Erina called back to Mizuki, who had stopped, staring, and then herself noticed Kurihara in the distance. 'Oh my God, she's really with the muumuu lady, isn't she? She's so weird.'

'What's she doing?' Mizuki asked.

'Who knows?' Erina said. 'I mean, it's just plain embarrassing, isn't it? I think she should take off the school uniform, at the very least.'

People around the clearly unusual duo glanced at them dubiously as they passed by.

Even without Erina saying so, Mizuki was embarrassed to be wearing the same uniform as Kurihara. This was really too much.

She was about to go and give them a piece of her mind, then she paused. Hadn't she just decided not to get involved with such people?

'Whoa, what's she doing with the old hag?' Kosaka was now standing next to them and, in a disgusted voice, joined in. 'Ugh. Totally hideous. I mean, awful.'

He pulled his phone from his pocket. Seeing him tap the camera, Mizuki said, 'Cut it out!' and stopped him. 'That's not right.'

'Huh? But why?' Kosaka pouted in dissatisfaction. 'It's hysterical, isn't it?'

'It's spying. That's not right.'

Even as she was speaking, she wondered why she had to explain this. Shouldn't it be obvious to any decent person with common sense?

'If you were still the Queen, you'd just order me to take the photo, and off with her head!'

'Sasuke, don't be such an idiot! No girl wants a photo like that.' Erina cackled. 'Girls only want beautiful things on their phones. Cute things.'

'Oh, for real? Who knew?'

'Maybe that's why you're still single. If you keep on like that, you might turn off Mizuki, too,' Erina added meaningfully, and Kosaka showed signs of panic.

'Whoa, definitely wouldn't want that.'

Mizuki pretended not to notice any of this. 'Let's just go and see the movie.' She spun on her heels and stalked off.

'Wait up, Mizuki!'

Hearing Kosaka's voice over Kurihara's laughter in the background irritated her somehow.

★

'Mizuki, you haven't been getting out of the house much lately, have you?'

At her mother Sumie's voice, Mizuki looked up from the magazine she was reading.

'Are you going to spend your whole Sunday lying around the living room? You used to go out much more often.'

Erina and her friends didn't live nearby, so Mizuki didn't spend much time with them on weekends. They weren't interesting enough for her to make the effort. Mostly, they only wanted to hang out with boys, and Mizuki didn't find that entertaining at all. Kosaka in particular seemed to have a crush on her and was too familiar when he addressed her, which was annoying since she wasn't interested in him.

Erina and the others didn't make much of an effort to invite her, either. They had all got along so well since middle school, the three of them, that they didn't seem to care whether or not Mizuki was there.

'Are you having trouble making new friends in high school?' Sumie asked.

'No, I have friends. We hang out after school sometimes, don't we? And then I come home.'

'That's true, I suppose. But the relationship with them seems a little shallow, doesn't it?'

Sumie had always had a sharp intuition regarding such things. Mizuki had never been able to lie to her mother. There had been times when she was happy that her mother seemed to know her inside and out, but right now it was just annoying.

'I'm telling you, that's not the problem at all! It's just they're trying to pair me up with a boy I don't like, so I don't want to see them when we're not in school uniform!'

That was half true, at least. She didn't want to see Kosaka in her regular clothes. He'd probably say something like 'Just what I expected!' or maybe 'I thought you'd be way more dressed up.' Either way, just the thought of having to respond to him was exhausting.

Her mother seemed to buy it, or, anyway, Sumie just frowned, and said, 'Don't waste your time on strange boys, all right?'

'Got it, Mother. I would never be that dumb.'

Mizuki didn't have a father. Or, to be precise, she had one, but her parents were separated. They had been on bad terms for as long as Mizuki could remember, and when she was five, her father had got another woman pregnant and left. He had wanted a divorce, but Sumie had refused – for Mizuki's sake, she had said – so now her father lived in another house with his mistress and their own child, just the three of them.

Men were such utterly useless creatures, Mizuki thought. What a woman needed in life was something she could rely on – not a man's love, but a woman's friendship. She had been told this at every opportunity as she grew older.

'You know I would only hang out with nice boys, Mother.'

'Right. That's good. Oh dear, if only you had made up with Azusa, you wouldn't have to worry about any of this nonsense now, would you? Her mother, Michiyo, was as sorry as I was. She couldn't understand how it came to all that, when you two were so close.'

'It wasn't me, Mother. It was Azusa who decided she didn't want to be friends with me anymore,' Mizuki shot back. 'How many times do I have to tell you?' She closed her magazine.

She'd tried to approach Azusa a number of times. She had even offered to forgive her. But Azusa had stubbornly refused to apologise.

'I don't even want to be friends with her anymore.'

'Well, that's as may be, but I think you should try to make some other nice friends. It seems like the spark's really gone out of you since you started high school. You really used to look forward to every single day,' Sumie said with a look of genuine disappointment, and Mizuki struggled to resist a rising tide of irritation.

Nobody was more frustrated than Mizuki about the loss of those happy days. There had certainly been times when she had looked forward to high-school life with eager anticipation, but now that she was actually living it, her heart just wasn't in it. It wasn't supposed to be like this, was all she could think.

'Maybe you can find a hobby? A skill to develop? Say, why don't you sign up for some extracurricular lessons in music or art? Actually, I heard that your father is sending his kid for English conversation lessons now. They're going to apply to private schools next year. Although he said public school was fine for you. What's different now, I wonder? So I figure there's no need to be shy about asking him to pay for lessons for you. After all, you're his real daughter.'

'I'm going out.'

Mizuki dropped the magazine and left the house quickly, taking only her phone and wallet.

Mizuki and her mother lived in an apartment with an ocean view. Her father ran a construction company, and although he did really want the divorce, he covered the living expenses of his legal wife and daughter faithfully, so the two of them had never run into financial trouble. Her mother worked in the office of a medical clinic and could never have hoped to afford such a place on her own wages.

Hearing her mother talk about her father's family always put Mizuki in a dark mood. Her father had a family of his own, one that he genuinely loved. So she couldn't help feeling that her whole life was a mistake.

However, Sumie had taken pains to raise her so that she never had to think of such things. Her mother had never formally separated from her father, and she made sure that he fulfilled the minimum obligations of fatherhood by providing for his daughter. Mizuki understood that this was evidence of her mother's sincere love, and she was grateful for it. People who didn't know her circumstances assumed she had been raised as the privileged daughter of a proper, two-parent home, and treated her accordingly. So it was thanks to her mother, Mizuki thought, that she was able to grow up without seeing herself as less worthy than others.

But when she thought about her father, whom she hadn't seen even once since the separation, she couldn't help but wonder if all that was actually for the best. Her existence wasn't important to him anymore. He may have retained some sense of responsibility towards her, but she was no longer his darling daughter.

During the winter of her third year in middle school, Mizuki had witnessed an encounter between her parents. She'd felt unwell one day and came home early from school, only to find her father at the house. Wondering if they were finally getting a divorce, she had quietly hidden herself to eavesdrop on the conversation unnoticed. Sumie, who was ordinarily always brisk and energetic, spoke with a tremor in her voice. 'You can forget about a divorce,' she said. 'I won't have them say our daughter is the child of a single-parent home. I won't have her saddled with that handicap. I don't want her to have to struggle with that. Blame me if you want, but we won't divorce. Mizuki is more important to me than your new child.'

'Forgive me,' her father had said in a miserable voice. 'I'll make sure Mizuki's needs are met. I'll even pay her university tuition. Now please, just let me go. Let me be Tatsuki's father. He won't even call me *Dad*, the way things are now!'

'That's your own fault, isn't it? Of the two of us, who do you think is in the right here?' Sumie had shouted. 'Don't you understand? This is about Mizuki, your legitimate daughter, not the child of an illicit affair! Which of them requires your support? You're the one who had an illegitimate child, not me. It's your fault he's in this situation. That's the truth, and you know it!'

Scared by this sudden fierceness, Mizuki had peeked out from her hiding place and saw Sumie's face, trembling and deathly pale. Mizuki had never seen her usually upbeat mother like this, and was speechless, while her father's shoulders sagged in defeat.

'You're right. I understand.'

That had been a bad day for Mizuki.

Out in the fresh air, she shook her head to clear it and mounted her bicycle. She hadn't wanted to talk anymore with her mother, so she had come outside, which was fine, but now – where should she go?

After thinking for a moment, she posted a message to a thread with six old friends from middle school. 'Who's free today?' she wrote. Then, 'Want to get a parfait at Moon?' Maybe if she got together with her old friends for a talk, she'd feel more like her old self. The girl her mother had been talking about, who still had a little spark in her.

Mizuki waited. She could see the message had been read by two friends, then a third, but there were no replies. She waited a little longer, and finally there was a ding from the phone. 'Sorry, working today.'

Two more messages quickly arrived.

'Out with parents.'

'Needed at home, sorry.'

This was new. As recently as a few months ago, Mizuki's messages would be marked read instantly and the group would gather without delay. Now it seemed like the others – including Kanako, who was probably closer to her than anyone else in middle school – hadn't even looked at the message. No matter how long Mizuki waited, the 'message read' markers didn't appear.

'Never mind. Another time,' Mizuki texted back quickly, then tossed the phone into her bike basket.

That's annoying, Mizuki thought, but started to pedal anyway.

Somehow, nothing was going right. All the pieces of her life that used to fit together so neatly seemed to be breaking apart all around her.

'I hate this. I really hate it,' she said out loud. But even having said so, she didn't know what to do about it.

Shortly after that, Mizuki discovered just how many pieces of her life were broken. It was when she arrived at Mojikō Station.

She saw Kanako entering the train station, laughing happily with the girls who had declined her invitation earlier. Were they going to Okura or some other fun neighbourhood in Kitakyūshū? Dressed for a friendly outing, they disappeared behind the station doors, chattering happily together.

'They're all here?' Mizuki mumbled. And it was true, they had all got together. But if they had invited her, she would have come too. So why had they turned her down? They had even lied.

Thinking back, Mizuki realised that they had hardly got together at all since they had left middle school. Lately, even the number of posts to their friend group had dropped precipitously. Once, she used to have her hands full just catching up on unread messages.

Maybe that couldn't be helped, since they went to different schools now. Mizuki had made new friends of her own, too, like Erina and her coterie. But that didn't mean her old friends had to exclude her like this.

Instantly, a tremendous surge of rage overtook her. She dropped her bicycle and charged into the train station. Kanako and her friends were about to place an order at the Starbucks counter.

'Hey! Hold on!' Mizuki shouted, and Kanako's face froze in shock when she recognised her.

'It's Mizuki!' squeaked Hitomi, the girl who had claimed to be with her parents, a note of terror in her voice.

'Why did you lie to me!' Mizuki glared at the group of girls. 'If you're going to lie and cut someone out like that, you better have a good reason!'

The girls fell silent. Then Kanako spoke.

'Because . . .' she said. 'Because we always have to watch ourselves around you.'

'Huh?' Mizuki said, taken aback. *Watch themselves?* What did that mean?

'You get so mad if things don't go the way you want. We just realised we're happier on our own, without you!'

'It . . . it's true,' Hitomi said. 'It's exhausting, being with you.'

Honoka nodded in agreement.

'What? You all think that?' Mizuki looked around at them, a slight tremor in her voice. She didn't know if it was due to anger or just plain shock. The ground seemed to be trembling beneath her feet.

The pretty barista behind the Starbucks counter gave Mizuki a troubled look. There seemed to be a note of pity in her expression.

'Once you weren't around anymore, we figured it out. We should have realised that it was wrong to have you controlling our lives all the time.' Kanako spoke firmly, as if steeling herself against a storm. 'We don't want to have to flatter and fawn over you, like you're royalty. So we can't hang out with you anymore. Bye now.'

Fawning? Had they been fawning over her? The sharpness of Kanako's words left Mizuki speechless.

Kanako turned back to the barista, still looking on in consternation, and said, 'Sorry about that. Can I order now?'

Emboldened by Kanako's little speech, Hitomi and Honoka in turn blurted out their own dismissals, faces averted.

'Me too, sorry.'

'I just can't anymore.'

With her former friends standing before her, acting like she wasn't even there, Mizuki could say nothing in response. She bit her lip tightly. And then, slowly, she turned and walked away. There was no way she was going to let them see her cry.

Fighting back tears as her vision blurred, Mizuki forced herself to walk calmly. She righted her fallen bicycle, pushing it ahead of her as she moved away. She had half an idea that someone would come running after her to say they were sorry, but wait as she would, the voice never came.

Once she had put some distance between her and the train station, the tears came in earnest. Why did they have to say such heartless things to her? When had she ever been that cruel to anyone? They had always respected her, hadn't they, because what she said was always right. Or had she been mistaken? And what was all that about fawning? She had never asked them to do anything like that.

I can't take it anymore, she thought, wiping away the tears. It was all just so suffocating. Nothing in middle school had been this hard. Every day went by just as she expected, and there was never a hint of sadness or anxiety.

'Here, now! What's wrong?'

A gruff voice came her way. Ahead of her was a stern-faced old man astride a red cargo bike. It was Old Red.

'What's all this blubbering? Are you hurt?'

He pedalled closer, his cargo bike squeaking with each revolution of the wheels, until he ground to a halt right in front of Mizuki. She stared at him in surprise. A white tank top and red overalls. Sturdy, jutting arms and bare head browned by the sun. He looked as if he had been cut from rough-hewn timber, and his white-bearded face had a positively ferocious look about it.

'Oh!' Mizuki replied, startled. 'No, I'm not . . .' Her voice was a little hoarse, perhaps from her tears.

'Crying on a hot day like this, you'll get dehydrated. You have something to drink, young lady?'

Mizuki shook her head. But as soon as she heard the words, she started to feel really thirsty. In addition to the tears still dampening her cheeks, she realised she was also sweating profusely.

'Your face is all red. No, this won't do at all. Let's see, now . . . ahh, I know. We'll go to the Tenderness.'

Old Red gestured with his chin, and Mizuki saw the Tenderness shop signpost.

'Oh, well . . . I can get there on my own, if I need to.'

'Nonsense! You're on the verge of heatstroke, young lady.' Old Red seized the bicycle that Mizuki had been pushing. 'I'll take this for you,' he said. 'Think you can walk that far? There's a place to rest at the Tenderness over there. Set yourself down a little and recover.'

Mizuki hadn't realised until she was told, but her head was spinning and her legs were unsteady. Even her breathing was a little irregular.

'S-sorry.'

'No matter, no matter. Just you walk, now.'

The sun was blazing hot. Summer had come so soon, thought Mizuki. How had that happened? It seemed like just yesterday that she had been attending the high-school opening assembly, feeling lonely because all her best friends weren't there. It was like the seasons had kept on marching forward but had left her behind, somehow.

Fresh tears welled up, and she wiped them away with the back of her hand.

'Hang in there now, missy, you'll make it,' said Old Red, and at the sound of his voice, Mizuki felt a little grateful.

The dine-in space at the Tenderness was pleasantly air-conditioned. Mizuki sat deep in a chair at a table for four, and drained a sports drink that Old Red had purchased for her. She could almost feel the cold liquid spreading through her body. She exhaled heavily, and Old Red handed her a second bottle.

'You'd best wear a hat when it's hot like today.'

'S-sorry. Thank you.'

Once Mizuki had collected herself, she started to feel a little embarrassed. She was no primary-school student. What was she thinking, walking around in tears, nearly giving herself heatstroke? And then, to think that she had to be rescued by Old Red!

'Um, I can pay for the drinks.'

'No need. Save your money for next time,' said the old man.

Mizuki looked at him askance. Did he mean that he expected to see her again?

But when she asked, he simply said, 'Use it the next time you see someone else in trouble. I believe in paying it forward. Caring and kindness get their value from sharing, see? That's how it is with such things.'

Old Red cackled.

When she was younger, Mizuki always used to think the man looked like a television villain when he laughed. In primary school, she'd run away if he so much as said *hello* to her. But looking at him now, she suddenly felt he had a kind of charm.

'Value from sharing . . .' Mizuki repeated to herself, looking from the old man to the empty bottles in front of her. She couldn't think of a soul with whom to share the care and kindness she had just received.

I guess I'm on my own. She chuckled ruefully to herself, and felt suddenly lonely, when a cheerful voice broke in.

'Hello! Whew, it's hot today, isn't it? I'm drenched!'

'Ah, hello there, young Shima! Why the outfit?' Old Red addressed the newcomer like an old friend.

Mizuki glanced over, and was surprised to see Kurihara standing there, wearing her school gym clothes. She was covered with mud and had a towel draped over her neck.

Kurihara grinned. 'I was Tsugi's assistant for the day. We've been up since dawn, collecting stag and rhinoceros beetles on Mount Hiko.' Her cheeks were flushed, perhaps from the sun.

'Shima did great.' A deeper voice broke in from behind Kurihara, and a dishevelled man with a shaggy beard appeared in the doorway. 'Kōsei and his pals came along on their bikes, but I swear she caught twice as many as all of them put together. She even plucked one right off her own back without looking! It's like she has a sixth sense.'

The bearded man was wearing a light green coverall, with the top half tied around his waist, exposing a white T-shirt and lean, muscular arms that looked skinny compared with Old Red's. Mizuki had the feeling she'd seen him somewhere before, but couldn't remember where. Where was it?

She cast her eyes around the room, and through the window she spotted a mini-truck with 'Whatever Guy' written on the side. Oh, that was it! She had seen him driving around town sometimes. He was a junk collector, something like that.

Of course, she thought. This must be the mysterious man in coveralls that Erina had said had been spotted with Kurihara.

'And tell me again why you're collecting the bugs?' said Old Red.

The man ran his fingers through his messy hair. 'One of the schoolteachers asked. So the kids can look after them.' He took an elastic band from his wrist and bound his hair back, neatly framing his eyes, which were hardly visible before. Mizuki was surprised to see his face, which was prettier than she had expected. If he lost the beard obscuring his lower face, she thought, he'd be quite handsome.

'It was really fun! Oh . . . Murai?' Kurihara, still smiling, noticed Mizuki looking at her in amazement. 'Wow, that's a surprise. I never thought I'd run into you somewhere like this! And you know Shōhei?'

Who was Shōhei? But before Mizuki could even begin to wonder about that, Old Red said, 'Well now! You know this little missy too, young Shima? She was near overcome with heatstroke, so I brought her here for a sit-down.'

'She's my classmate! But heatstroke, that sounds bad. Are you okay, Murai?'

Kurihara leaned in to look at her. Mizuki could see leaves stuck in the girl's hair, and smell her perspiration, as well as the musky odour of earth. There was something overwhelmingly powerful about her, not what Mizuki expected from a girl who usually vanished into the background when they were in class.

'Oh? You're Shima's friend? From school? Nice to meet you. I'm Tsugi.' With a glint of white teeth, the bearded man smiled at Mizuki.

'Um, yes, likewise.'

Mizuki responded, but looked at Kurihara. She wanted to ask her why she was so friendly with these men, said to be two of Mojikō's oddest characters. For a girl who had moved here just a handful of months earlier, it was certainly unexpected.

'Do you live in this neighbourhood, Murai?' Kurihara didn't seem to notice Mizuki's confusion.

Mizuki responded in the affirmative.

Kurihara replied, 'That must be nice,' then sighed. 'I'm actually really jealous. I've looked around and seen lots of different places since we moved here, but I like this neighbourhood best.'

Kurihara gave Mizuki a light-hearted smile. Her two front teeth were a little larger than the rest, and Mizuki thought it made her look a little like a squirrel.

'Mr Shōhei and Mr Tsugi are here, and I really like the Tenderness store, too. I think I would have been happy to come to Kyushu just for the Tenderness alone, but especially for this one. The store manager and everyone who works here are all so amazing.'

Mizuki hadn't really stopped to think about where she was, but once she had taken a good look around, she remembered that this particular shop was where the big fight with Azusa had taken place. Azusa – who knew her better than anyone in the world – had been meeting here secretly, with none other than Nayuta. Azusa couldn't possibly know how shocked Mizuki had been to come upon the two of them there, chatting away so happily. It hurt her, even more than when she learned her father had another child. It had felt like her whole world had come crashing down. Her mother had told her time and again that friendship was the only unbreakable thing in the world, so how could that have happened?

Now that she thought about it, Old Red and this Tsugi guy might have been present back then, too, but her memories of that day were already hazy. It was like someone had splashed bright red paint here and there, obscuring parts of the story, and she could only recall the remaining details in bits and pieces. Probably because it had been such an explosive, emotional day.

'The Tenderness is such a great place,' Kurihara added brightly. 'Especially the sweets here – they're so good.'

In response, Mizuki asked, 'But why are you here, Kurihara? Catching rhinoceros beetles, you said. Why would you want to do that?'

'It sounded interesting,' Kurihara said simply. She grinned again. 'I made up my mind that if something interests me, I'm just going to try it. And this seemed interesting, so I talked to Tsugi about it, and we got to be friends, yeah?'

'She just came right up to me and asked if I'd be her friend. Out of the blue.' Tsugi chuckled. 'I was pretty surprised at first, but she said she wanted to get to know all sorts of people, so I introduced her to Old Red, there.'

'That's right. Most of these youngsters seem to find me a tad intimidating. This was the first time one of 'em asked to be friends. Young Shima's a good kid, plenty curious.'

'And she's pretty interesting herself,' Tsugi added.

'Well, spending time with fun people like you two helps a person to grow, that's for sure,' Kurihara replied, glowing a little with pride. Then she turned back to Mizuki. 'Anyway, Murai, you always seem a little bored. Why is that? In class, I mean. Like maybe you're a little disappointed, yeah? So I was just wondering.'

'What? But you hardly know me at all!' Mizuki replied sharply, without stopping to think. Mizuki and Kurihara had basically just met. What right did the girl have to call her bored or anything like that?

Kurihara just looked at her quizzically. 'But we're in the same class every day. I haven't missed a day of school yet, and I think it's the same for you, isn't it? It's about six hours in class per day, okay? That's a decent amount of time to spend in the same room together. And then – do you remember three days ago? When Miss Hayashi got all stirred up in morning registration?'

Mizuki nodded. She did remember. For some reason, Miss Hayashi had been a little lacklustre throughout the previous week. She seemed slightly subdued, or maybe depressed, but then on Thursday morning she was all smiles. Her voice was stronger, she had a little glow about her, and even her expression was different. Erina had asked, 'Miss Hayashi, did you just make up with a boyfriend?' To which Miss Hayashi had replied something like, 'Not a boyfriend, but I got a pick-me-up from someone special.' Mizuki remembered someone saying that she had probably gone to some concert or play.

'You know who she was talking about?' Mizuki asked.

'Miss Hayashi has a crush on the store manager here.' Kurihara giggled a little as she spoke. 'She came on a visit to Mojikō about a year ago. She happened to drop into this Tenderness branch, and fell for the store manager at first sight, okay? She couldn't see him all last week, so when she finally came on Wednesday, it put her in a really good mood.'

'Eh?' Old Red said. 'I might know the woman.'

'She's in her thirties,' Kurihara said. 'She's beautiful, yeah? With really pretty black hair, and she always wears a white shirt and a straight black skirt.'

'We get a lot of pretty women at this store,' Old Red growled. 'Too many pretty women!'

'Wait, wait – are you saying the store manager is Miss Hayashi's boyfriend?' Mizuki asked, incredulously. 'I thought she didn't have a boyfriend!'

'The store manager here doesn't have a regular girlfriend, okay?' Kurihara responded. 'Miss Hayashi is just one of his fans.'

'Hmm . . . Just a fan?'

'I've been coming to the neighbourhood a lot lately, and I would see her around all the time. Eventually, I realised she was a regular, yeah? She's really into the store manager. I heard she's even thinking of moving to Mojikō, so she can see him lots more.'

This was a total surprise to Mizuki. She hadn't thought of Miss Hayashi as someone to be swayed by romantic entanglements. If anything, in fact, she was more likely to have a man wrapped around her little finger. So how could she imagine relocating just because she liked a guy she wasn't even dating!

'Oh! Then that's what was going on in class the other day, maybe?'

Miss Hayashi had reacted with some intensity when Kurihara had said something or other about the new Tenderness product line. Was it possible that she wasn't annoyed by one of her students talking nonsense, but instead excited to get the news? No, that couldn't be . . .!

'I don't believe it. Miss Hayashi's not like that.'

'See for yourself. I'll show you, okay?'

Kurihara extended a hand to Mizuki, who hesitantly took it. Ordinarily, she would have swatted it away, thinking how ridiculous the whole situation was. For starters, she had no interest at all in her teacher's love life, and furthermore, she would have been angry with Miss Hayashi for letting a romance interfere with her work. But she had been caught in a moment of weakness.

Hands linked, they entered the store through the side door from the dine-in space.

'Welcome,' said a gentle voice, and Mizuki saw a man standing behind the checkout counter. He looked like a model, and smiled at them pleasantly. The smile was gracious enough, but somehow it also felt a little too much.

'Psst . . . that can't be the guy, can it?'

'Bingo.' Kurihara laughed quietly, and spoke in a low voice. 'You're not into him, are you? Me neither. He's really nice and a totally wonderful person, okay? But there's something that's just too intense about him. It's like drinking noodle soup concentrate, or dousing yourself in Chanel perfume. It's just too strong.'

'Like drinking plum syrup without mixing it with anything.'

'That's it, exactly. You wouldn't think it to look at her, okay? But I heard Miss Hayashi really likes spicy food and strong drinks, so I figure the store manager's intense energy goes down well with her.'

Kurihara spoke with such assurance, and in spite of herself, Mizuki smiled. 'I can see it. You make a pretty good point there.' Their teacher was always so cool, calm and collected in the classroom. It was kind of fun to uncover this unexpected aspect to her.

'Anyway, you see what I mean, right?' Kurihara gave Mizuki a long, significant look. 'For a long time, we've been sitting in the same room, looking at the same person, okay? We share the same stories about her, we laugh together. I don't think you can say I don't know you at all.'

Mizuki had the sudden feeling that she'd been swept up in a pleasant breeze.

'There's lots I don't know about you, Murai, but there are a few things that I know for sure. Like how you stand so straight and tall when you walk that it makes you the most beautiful girl in class, and how your handwriting on the blackboard is really big and easy to read – silly things like that, but I do know them, okay?'

Kurihara smiled, momentarily revealing her big front teeth. Her pink glasses gleamed. Mizuki felt as if she were seeing her for the very first time. This girl who she had dismissed as a mere oddball hunched over her desk had just popped vividly into view.

'Well . . . should we buy some drinks?'

Kurihara turned and headed to the beverage aisle. She grabbed four bottles of tea and beelined to the counter. Startled, Mizuki hurried after her.

The store manager, whose name tag read 'Shiba', addressed Kurihara. 'Did you catch any rhinoceros beetles?' His voice slipped around Mizuki's ears in a way that gave her goosebumps.

'I sure did! Mr Tsugi said I was the best.'

'Well, then! Praise from that one doesn't come easy. You must have impressed him.'

The shop manager chuckled and the corners of his eyes crinkled kindly. He didn't seem like a bad guy at all. Still, there was something about him that made Mizuki uncomfortable. An aura, like static electricity, but totally different. Mizuki took a step back.

'I get it. With this guy I can see how Miss Hayashi might be affected,' Mizuki said quietly to Kurihara.

'I know! Lots of people come here just to see him.'

Juggling the four bottles of tea, Kurihara returned to the dine-in space, Mitzuki following close behind.

'Here you go!' she said, handing a bottle each to Tsugi and Old Red.

'It's hot, so drink up, everyone!' said Old Red.

'But you shouldn't have,' said Tsugi.

Kurihara just responded, 'You always treat me. I'm just returning the favour. I get to hear a lot of interesting stories from both of you, and it's always fun. And Tsugi paid me for helping today, so you can at least let me buy the drinks, okay?'

'Go around spending like that and you won't have anything to show for your day's work.'

'I wasn't helping for the money, anyway. Here, Murai, this one's for you, okay?' Kurihara held out a bottle to her classmate.

Mizuki looked at the bottle, damp with condensation from the warmth of Kurihara's arm. 'I can't accept that,' she said. 'I didn't do anything to earn it.'

'Well . . . how about if you say hello to me? Tomorrow, at school, okay?' Kurihara spoke hesitantly, as if slightly embarrassed. 'If you could, just *Good morning, Shima!* would be enough. I'd like that.'

Are you kidding me? Mizuki almost said it out loud, but Kurihara seemed perfectly serious. There was a gleam of hope in her eyes. As if impelled by that look, Mizuki accepted the bottle of tea.

In response, Kurihara's eyes lit up. 'Oh, thank you!'

'Don't make a big thing out of it. It's just a hello, right?'

'Right, just a hello. It's just saying hello!' Kurihara grinned.

Old Red leaned forward. 'Put the two bottles I bought you towards that as well. Hello to young Shima for two extra days.'

'Huh?' Mizuki frowned. 'But didn't you say you wanted me to pay it forward to someone else?' This was making no sense at all.

Old Red responded, 'But you've got no one else in mind, do you?'

'Um . . . well, that's true, I guess.'

Could he tell that? Mizuki was a little put off by the man's gruff manner, but Kurihara quickly said, 'Three days, then!' and seemed so pleased that Mizuki thought, *Well, why not?* But she was a strange girl, that was for sure. Just saying hello? What was the point?

'Okay, well, see you tomorrow. I'd better get home. Now that I've rested a little, I think I feel a headache coming on.' In fact, Mizuki could feel a sharp pain beginning to move from her temples to the back of her eyes. She had always been subject to headaches after any kind of physical distress. 'Sorry I have to go, but thanks for helping me today.'

She bowed to Old Red, who responded with an easy grin and said, 'It was nothing. Take care, now.'

'I will, thank you.'

Mizuki bowed to Tsugi as well, then left the building. The strong sunlight made her head spin just a little. She shook it slightly, then hopped on her bicycle and started pedalling for home.

The plastic bottle of tea rattled in the bike basket where Mizuki had placed it. An image of Kurihara and her smiling face appeared in her mind.

'What a strange girl,' she said.

Kurihara was by far and away the strangest kid Mizuki had ever met. And they had been in the same class all this time! It seemed a wonder that Mizuki hadn't become curious about her earlier.

I'll have to be sure to say good morning to her tomorrow, Mizuki thought, *and if it makes her that happy, I'll be sure to call her by her first name. Shima.* With that in mind, Mizuki began to pedal with a little more energy.

That evening, Mizuki received a phone call from Kosaka.

'I don't remember giving you my number,' she said.

Mizuki didn't waste time on texts and social networks with anyone but her closest friends. Personal time should be meaningful, she thought, not just frittered away on random people. That would be pointless. So she had never given Kosaka her contact info, no matter how often he'd asked, since he was just a friend of a friend.

'I got your details from Erina,' Kosaka responded, undeterred. 'What are you doing now?'

'Just reading.'

In truth, Mizuki had been lying in bed, staring blankly at the ceiling. When she'd got home, she had checked the message group that she had created with Kanako and the others, and everyone except for Mizuki was gone. They had all ditched the group, and Mizuki herself was now the only name remaining under 'Close Friends'. The tears that she thought she had completely exhausted earlier in the day had started to flow again. Did they really have to shut her out so completely . . .?

But she certainly didn't want to share anything like this with Kosaka. Making a conscious effort to sound normal, she mentioned the title of the latest hot novel, which had been hailed as a masterpiece. Seemingly oblivious to her mood, he responded broadly, 'Nope, never heard of it. Sounds way too hardcore for me. But okay, Mizuki, you've got a serious side too, don't you?'

'How serious I am has nothing to do with it. I just read what I like.' Erina and the others had known Kosaka for years, so she tried to be a little nicer to him in front of them. But now she didn't need to hold back. 'So, what do you want?'

'Huh? Oh. Well, um . . . do you want to go out with me?' Suddenly, Kosaka sounded a little self-conscious. 'We've been hanging out with everyone a lot lately, and you're super cute and sweet, too, and I like you for real.'

Mizuki could hear a faint whistle in the background on Kosaka's end. Was someone else there with him?

'I think we could be really good together. Like Erina and Atsushi. So let's go out.'

Another whistle. And then voices. It sounded like there were a few people there. *Oh!* Mizuki suddenly thought. Maybe they were – or no, there was no maybe about it. They were definitely getting a kick out of this. The thought was so shocking that Mizuki went blank for a second.

Not sure what to make of her silence, Kosaka said, 'Mizuki? Did I catch you off guard? Maybe you're feeling a little shy. If you are, that's really cute!' He sounded almost giddy.

Mizuki could hear the others hooting and hollering around him. She felt humiliated. Another tear rolled down her cheek. It was all just too much, the shock of this on top of what had happened earlier.

I don't deserve to be treated like this. I don't deserve to be hurt this way.

'No . . .' Her voice came slowly.

'What do you mean?' Kosaka said lightly, still a little giddy.

'No way.' She spoke slowly, but clearly.

'Huh?' Kosaka gasped. 'What . . . I mean, why . . . Did you just turn me down?' Now he was completely flustered.

'I said no. No way,' Mizuki repeated.

She heard a quick exchange on the other end of the line, and the voice on the phone changed.

'Hi Mizuki, this is Atsushi. Is everything cool there? Did we throw you for a little loop?'

Suddenly, Yoshikawa's laid-back tone was getting on Mizuki's nerves.

'Listen, Mizuki, Sasuke likes you for real,' Yoshikawa continued. 'He's always goofing around, so he may be a little too forward sometimes, but he's actually a good guy. You can trust him. I promise.'

Mizuki wiped the tears from her face and took a deep breath. 'I said no,' she repeated. 'Kosaka is just a friend, nothing more. That's how I feel.'

'But you might get to like him once you know him better, right?'

'I can't. Not when he plays around with someone's feelings this way.'

I could never date someone who treated me so carelessly, Mizuki thought.

'What?' Yoshikawa's tone shifted. 'What did he do wrong? What's wrong with rooting for a friend when he bares his heart? My pals were right by my side when I told Erina how I felt about her, you know!'

'Erina may have been happy about that, but it doesn't mean that I like that sort of thing. I think it's really rotten of you all. And if Kosaka thinks that a creepy come-on like that is going to make me happy, then it's hard to believe he even likes me at all.'

'I don't get it, Mizuki. Don't you think you're going overboard?'

That may have been true. Mizuki understood that. She had been angry. But if Kosaka had made his advances with a little more respect for her feelings, she wouldn't have said anything like that. She still wouldn't have gone out with him, that was for sure, but she would have said she was sorry, and let him down as gently as possible.

'It really annoys me that he'd go behind my back to get my number. I don't like it when people share my details without asking. Sorry, but I'm not going out with him.'

'Hey. Stop it. If you're going to treat my friend like that, I'll make sure you have nothing to do with Erina anymore. Understand?'

'Erina knew that Kosaka was going to call me like this, didn't she? She knew, and she just stood by and watched, didn't she? So that doesn't change anything.'

Oh. Starting tomorrow, I'm going to be on my own now, at school. The thought flashed through Mizuki's mind, but she steeled herself, and spoke with determination.

'Well, goodbye,' she said, and ended the conversation. Her heart was pounding and her hands were trembling slightly. 'Oh, it's true. I *did* go overboard, didn't I?'

She felt a slight stab of regret. But then, she couldn't let someone treat her that way. That was that. And even if she had agreed to go out with Kosaka, they would surely have pulled something like this on her again sometime.

'Ugh.'

Mizuki's phone pinged. A message had arrived in the group chat for Erina and her friends. Then the pings continued, as more messages arrived, flowing in continuously, one after another.

'You don't make fun of a person's boyfriend!'

'I like Sasuke, so I can't forgive that.'

'For real, Ami? You should go to him. He's hurting for sure, turned down by such a horrible person.'

'You should! By the way, Mizuki, you're really the worst.'

'Don't even try to talk to us tomorrow.'

'That's right. It's over. And delete this group. You're out.'

Mizuki put down her phone with a sigh. She didn't want to go to school tomorrow. But if she really couldn't stand being cut off by Erina and the others, then, ultimately, she'd have to change schools anyway. So, she didn't have much choice.

'What have I done?' Mizuki said to herself.

★

The next day, clutching her aching stomach, she left the house. She rode her bike to the station and boarded the train, swaying as it began to move. She had put a cold compress on her face before going to sleep last night, but her eyelids still felt heavy and slightly swollen. She didn't want anyone to know how hurt she was.

Oh, I don't want to go to school.

As Mizuki stepped off the train, her eyes panned down along the crowd on the station platform, and then, softly, she took a breath.

In the distance, there stood Azusa.

She went to a different school, so there was no reason for her childhood friend to be here. Why was she?

Automatically, Mizuki looked around, and noticed a number of kids wearing the same school uniform as Azusa. They were all carrying large shoulder bags, and Mizuki wondered if they were headed off to camp or some sort of similar activity.

'Azusa . . .'

Azusa, listen. Everyone's being so hard on me. Even though I only said what was right, they all ditched me, now nobody will talk to me. Tell me why, won't you?

Out of the blue, the words that Azusa had thrown at her a year before came back to her: *The day may come when someone responds with even more anger, or even violence.*

Mizuki had been shocked by the changes in her friend, and wanted things back to the way they were. So she had demanded that Azusa apologise, and that was the reply. At that time, she had been so outraged by Azusa's words that she'd almost slapped her, but had frozen mid-swing, hand in the air.

What stayed her hand was Azusa's unbroken gaze, looking steadily into her eyes. In that gaze there was no hint of mockery or belittlement, nothing like that. She was just hoping with all her heart that nothing like that would ever happen to Mizuki.

Azusa was quickly moving farther away down the platform, laughing and talking with one of her classmates. And her figure was becoming blurry with tears.

Azusa. Whose hopes for Mizuki back then hadn't come true. Whose words, if Mizuki had listened to them properly, would have ensured that things would be different now.

'I'm sorry, Azusa.'

Mizuki spoke quietly to Azusa as she disappeared into the crowd, and as she did, she felt a sharp blow, smack in the centre of her back. She spun around, and found herself face to face with Erina and her friends, all of them wearing smug grins. Erina was holding a gym bag, with which she had apparently struck Mizuki.

'Don't just stand there staring like an idiot. You're in the way! I'm surprised you're even willing to show your face at school,' Erina added mockingly, then stepped around Mizuki and walked past, followed by the others.

Ami turned back suddenly, and laughed. 'I'm going out with Sasuke, just so you know. He said he was glad he didn't fall for your looks when there was such a horrible person underneath.'

'I mean, she's not even that cute! She just acts like she is.'

The three of them walked off, chattering.

Mizuki's back hurt. Feeling the pain, she suddenly wondered about her own behaviour.

Have I been doing the very same thing?

When things didn't go her way, when someone behaved in a way that didn't make sense to her – did she dismiss people too easily? Did she criticise them too loudly?

Yes, Mizuki could see it now. She was guilty of all of that. She had never considered the feelings or circumstances of the people in her sights. And if she did learn someone's story, she felt annoyance, not sympathy. It was their job to explain themselves, she thought, if they wanted others to understand.

So that's how it is. This is what it took to open my eyes?

What a fool she had been, not to understand this until she was in the same situation herself.

When Mizuki finally got to school, the mood in the classroom was different. She looked around and said good morning to a few people. Ordinarily, she received a cheerful response, but today everyone looked away awkwardly, or at best gave a quick, perfunctory 'hi'. Unsure of how to handle this, Mizuki took her seat, but as she did, a mocking voice rang out: 'The bully has arrived!'

Looking around, she saw Erina and her friends, heads together, snickering.

'Someone who went to her middle school told me Mizuki was a big bully there. Is that true, Mizuki? We heard you even forced another student to switch schools!'

'It wasn't like that!'

Nayuta had just moved to be with her mother's family.

But Erina continued. 'I think it was exactly like that. Everyone I talked to says you bullied a girl who was trying so hard to care for her dying mother. That you told her she had to be polite to you, and that you told everyone else to avoid her. That's so messed up!'

'That's not what I did. She just didn't say hello, and then the other girls—'

'Oh, that's right! You didn't do anything, did you? You just had your followers do it for you, right? Like the

Queen of Hearts!' Erina turned to Ami, standing next to her, and said in an exaggerated tone, 'Hop to it! Off with her head!'

Ami laughed. 'No! The Queen of Hearts? What a joke! Actually, it's so pathetic.'

'Listen, I didn't mean to do anything like that. I don't remember telling anyone to do anything at all. And besides, I didn't know about her family situation, anyway.'

'Oh, so it's okay to bully someone if you don't know them?'

That wasn't it at all. But . . . Mizuki didn't know what else to say.

She looked around the room, but everywhere she looked, faces turned awkwardly away. *Ah. Nobody is going to help me*, Mizuki realised. She had never felt so hopeless before.

'There's no excuse for bullying, no matter what the reason,' Erina said. 'It's unforgivable, isn't it? So we can't forgive you.' Somehow, both the expression on her face and her tone of voice reminded Mizuki of herself.

Oh, she thought. *So that was the old me. I hurt other people this way. I'm sorry, Nayuta. I'm so sorry, Azusa. But even when I was causing you all that pain, you held your heads high, didn't you? I don't think I'll be able to do that . . .*

'Mizuki! Good morning!' Just then, a cheerful, carefree voice rang out. Kurihara was standing at the classroom door. Her arm was raised high in an eager salute.

Ami let out a snort of derision.

Saori said mockingly, 'Oh, this is just too good!'

The rest of the class were watching Kurihara with varying degrees of amusement. But Kurihara maintained her laser focus on Mizuki.

'Um, listen, Kurihara. We're kind of having an important conversation right now—'

Erina started to speak, visibly annoyed, but Kurihara just ploughed on, repeating in an even louder voice, 'Mizuki! Good morning!'

Kurihara's cheeks were ever so slightly pink. Her eyes shone eagerly, as if she were making an appeal.

Oh, thought Mizuki. *She's nervous too.* How much courage it must have taken, just to say so much as *hello* in that atmosphere!

Mizuki stood up and waved, although perhaps not quite as enthusiastically as Kurihara.

'K-Kuri . . . No, wait.' Mizuki decided to use Kurihara's given name. 'Er, good morning, Shima!'

Kurihara's face brightened instantly. She scampered over to Mizuki like an eager puppy, saying 'Good morning!' one more time for good measure.

'You remembered your promise! I'm glad!'

'I'm not silly enough to forget something like that,' Mizuki said, trying to laugh, but unable to conceal the tremor in her voice. Her face felt frozen, as well. She realised full well that she had just been rescued by this strange girl. 'Well, um . . .' She didn't know what to say. What did one do at a time like this?

Mizuki opened her mouth, then hesitated, and Kurihara's face swiftly clouded over. Then, as if making up her mind, Kurihara nodded once firmly, took Mizuki by the hand and gave a vigorous tug. 'This way!'

'Kurihara. Do you mind? You're getting in the way.' Now Erina made no effort to conceal her displeasure. Mizuki looked at Erina, who jerked her chin towards the other girl and said, 'Do something about that. What's with her, anyway? Kurihara, can't you read the room? We're busy here.'

Kurihara whirled on Erina. She took a deep breath, then suddenly said, 'No! You read it! Can't you see that *we're* busy? We don't require your company right now!'

Her voice was loud enough that she was practically shouting. Mizuki was speechless, and Erina's eyes nearly popped out of her head.

Kurihara turned back to Mizuki. 'Let's go!' She ran out of the classroom, dragging the bewildered Mizuki with her.

'Wait, what? What are we doing?' Mizuki stammered, but Kurihara didn't loosen her grip. She tugged her along until they reached the school doors.

'Put on your outdoor shoes,' Kurihara said, then led Mizuki straight through the school gate!

'Wait, wait . . . but we have class!'

'It doesn't matter!'

Mizuki was flustered, but she couldn't free herself from Kurihara's grip. And, in truth, she had wanted to leave. She had been hoping against hope for someone to come along and rescue her from the awful situation. So whatever Kurihara might be up to, maybe it suited her fine.

They made their way to a small park, and Kurihara finally let go of Mizuki's hand. She found a bench and, gesturing to Mizuki, said, 'Sit,' and then sat beside her.

The two of them were alone in the park, with the exception of a few pigeons a small distance away, bobbing their heads as they walked this way and that. A cool morning breeze threaded its way between them. They had run most of the way from school and Mizuki was perspiring, so the air felt pleasantly refreshing as it played over her skin. Kurihara sat with her two fists clenched in her lap, staring at them fixedly. Her thin, childlike shoulders rose and fell with each breath.

'Well, um . . .' After a brief silence, Mizuki was about to speak, but Kurihara was faster.

'I'm sorry!' she blurted out, bowing her head in a forceful apology. 'I'm sorry. It's just like Erina said. I can't read the room!'

'What?'

'I'm not really good at picking up on certain things, yeah? And I tend to panic. You looked really uncomfortable before, like you just wanted to leave, so all I could think about was getting you out of there. Was that bad? Did I make a mistake? I'm really sorry!' Kurihara's face had turned red. 'Listen, if I did the wrong thing, just tell me. We can go back to school, I can apologise to Erina. I can even tell the teacher that I dragged you away.'

She looked up at Mizuki, her eyes hesitant and slightly damp, almost on the verge of tears. All Mizuki could think of was how beautiful they were.

'Hey, can I ask you something?' Mizuki said impulsively. 'Did you really do all that for me just because I looked uncomfortable? We were only together for a short time yesterday. I know we've been in the same class all this time, doing the same things together like you said, but I still don't know you that well. So I don't understand why you worked so hard to get me out of there. Will you explain it to me?'

Suddenly, Kurihara lowered her eyes. In a small voice, she said, 'I just . . . I just wanted a friend.'

The answer was so simple.

'I thought, if I want to be friends with someone, I have to do something for them.'

At first, Mizuki was surprised, but then she thought, *Oh, that's right, when I was younger I dealt with people that way, too.* She wanted a lot of friends and to spend her time happily surrounded by them. She wanted them all to like her, so she thought she had to do something to earn each and every friend. She thought that she had to try extra hard for Azusa.

'People always tell me I'm a little different. I did have friends in Tokyo, but it wasn't easy, and it took time. I was pretty sure I wouldn't be able to do that again. So I didn't want to move to Kyushu, but my dad didn't want to be transferred away without his family, so that was that.'

Apparently, Kurihara's father was a 'family first' kind of man, the type who thought parents and children should take all their meals together at the table. So when they started talking about a transfer at work, it went without saying that the entire family would have to relocate.

'My mother and my older brother told him that it would be hard on me. That I'd be all on my own at the new school. But my dad wouldn't budge. He didn't listen to them, the family moved here, and I did have trouble making friends, just like we thought. Whenever I tried to talk to anyone, they'd give me a polite smile and just walk away. I was on my own every day, and I had nobody to talk to. I was so lonely. I would spend the whole day watching everyone in the classroom talk to each other, but it felt like I had become completely invisible.'

As Kurihara told her story, Mizuki thought back over her own recollections of the year in class, but try as she might, she couldn't picture Kurihara in any of them. She was there, of course, but Mizuki had been totally unaware of her presence. She felt a sharp pang of regret about overlooking her so completely for so long. Kurihara had obviously noticed her.

'But then, you know, I met Tsugi, and since then I've been having so much fun.' Kurihara's voice brightened. 'I'm glad I met him. He really changed everything.'

'How did you meet?' Mizuki asked.

'I just spoke to him,' Kurihara replied. 'I was at Aru-Aru City, the mall by Kokura Station. Near the bullet train entrance? There was a mini-truck parked in front, with a logo that said *Whatever Guy*, and Mr Tsugi was standing nearby. He was wearing a coverall with the same logo, so I got curious and asked him what kind of work he did. And he said, "I do whatever, so I'm the Whatever Guy." So I asked him if he'd be my friend.'

'Really? But that could have been dangerous! What if he had been some kind of creep?'

At Mizuki's shocked tone, Kurihara thought for a moment, and then quietly replied, 'I guess that's what people mean when they say someone's grasping at straws. I didn't even think about that. Or, no, maybe I didn't even care. Anyway, I'm glad I talked to him. Mr Tsugi isn't creepy at all, he just has a strong personality. I think he's really unique. So I got curious about what kind of experiences he's had, and now I'm totally fascinated by him. Like, what kind of life do you think he's led, to end up the way he is? I'm so dull in comparison, like a watered-down soda. What do you think it would take for someone like me to be like that?'

Kurihara's voice grew warmer, as if a switch had been flipped somewhere.

'Lately, I've been trying to stick close to Mr Tsugi when I have free time, so I can take notes when he talks about his past or says something interesting, so I can try to understand it. It's like a research project. Every little thing about him is just so deep. And then, in the middle of that I was introduced to Mr Shōhei, and I just thought, wow, here's an even stronger personality. Mr Shōhei is really great. I'm fascinated by him, too. I want to know why he calls himself Mojikō's tourism ambassador, what his family is like, what kind of life he's led. He's so dramatic! And I'm interested in the store manager, also, but remember how we were saying he was like Chanel perfume? Well, whatever it is, I think I'm probably not ready for that, so I'm keeping my distance for now. And another cool person is Miss Itoko! She's this really stylish lady who's always walking around Cha-Cha Town, but she used to be a dance teacher for modern ballet. She's worked with really famous actresses!'

'Okay, wait a minute . . .' Mizuki, listening dumbfounded as Kurihara rattled on faster and faster, was beginning to have trouble following. 'I'm listening carefully, but you have to slow down. Um, so basically, you met Tsugi, you thought he was interesting, and then, through him, you met some more cool friends?'

As Mizuki summed up the story, Kurihara said, 'Oh . . . yes! That's it, exactly.' Apparently, Kurihara spoke faster when she got excited, and her verbal tics disappeared as well. Mizuki was surprised to find herself thinking this was kind of cute. In the past, she probably would have been irritated by such a vague personality quirk. *If you can forget to do it, just stop doing it*, she would have thought. 'It's true. I met so many wonderful friends. Oh, wait – I mean, I did meet them. So I thought I didn't need to make any more friends, but everyone keeps telling me that I need friends my own age, the kind I can build a deep connection with.'

Realising she'd omitted her trademark phrase, Kurihara

continued awkwardly, searching for the right words. In life, we go through good times and bad, she explained, and it's nice to have a friend one's own age to share the experiences and reflect upon them together. Best not to rush things, though – just keep on the lookout. And then, when the time is right, start talking. That's what everyone had told her. Why she'd been searching all this time.

Aha, so yesterday, it was that time, thought Mizuki. When Kurihara had handed her that bottle of tea, making her odd request, it was all because the time was right. And then Old Red, what he'd asked in return for the two bottles he had given Mizuki, that was a gift, to his friend Kurihara . . .

'When I first met you, you were with Shōhei-san and Tsugi-san. So I thought, *This must be the one*. That it was destiny,' Kurihara explained.

'Destiny? That's a bit strong.'

'Right, maybe a bit strong. But that's how I felt, yeah? And from the way you're listening to me now, I'm thinking maybe I wasn't so far off.'

Kurihara gave a brief laugh.

'Oh. But then, maybe you don't want to be friends. Everyone laughs at me just for talking, so I guess it might be pretty embarrassing for you.'

'Please, don't . . .'

Mizuki struggled to hold back her tears. It wouldn't be right for her to start crying at this point, she thought.

A year ago, Mizuki would have scorned Kurihara as some kind of weirdo. She would have thought that a classmate who hung out with the likes of the Whatever Guy and Old Red meant trouble. She would have condemned her, and tried to ostracise her. In fact, she had done that.

But Kurihara had saved her. There was nothing 'weird' or 'risky' about the way she lived or thought. She just put her whole self into every day, trying her hardest to get by.

'I think I'm going to be pretty unpopular with our class from now on.' It would have been dishonest of Mizuki not to admit it, so she just said it. 'Erina and the rest of them don't like me at all now. Also, I think you should know that I used to be pretty rotten. People like you . . . well, I bullied them.'

Mizuki choked on the words. She was forced to admit it. What she had done to Taguchi Nayuta was bullying, and no mistake. She had brandished a sword in the name of justice, but really she had just been taking pleasure from taking others to task.

'I did terrible things. I'm a terrible person. And now I'm paying the price for it. There's nothing good about being my friend.'

A single tear from the flood Mizuki was holding back escaped, tracing a line down her cheek. The fists she had unknowingly made trembled in her lap.

'There's no one who hasn't done something terrible at least once in their life,' Kurihara said reflectively. 'And that goes for me, too. When I was in fourth grade, I stole something from our local general store. I was invited to a friend's birthday for the first time, and I wanted to bring a present, but I had no allowance, so I stole a container of solid perfume. It smelled like soap.'

A store employee noticed the theft immediately, Kurihara told Mizuki, and her teacher and mother were called. Kurihara and her mother bowed repeatedly and pleaded for mercy, and because Kurihara had never done anything like this before the shopkeeper let her go.

'But my teacher got really mad and made a terrible face. He said it was deplorable, that he had thought better of me. Also that it was unforgiveable, the worst thing someone could do. And I thought he was right. I was so ashamed of myself that I wanted to disappear forever. After my teacher left and I was going home with my mother, I started to cry and told her how sorry I was. And my mother said only that if I was truly sorry, I would never do it again. *Children are immature creatures*, she said. *They make many mistakes and sometimes do the wrong thing, so we should never scold them the first time round. Instead, we encourage them to feel regret and reflect upon their actions, and to be sure it doesn't happen again. That's how a person becomes an adult.*'

Kurihara was sharing a precious memory with her. Mizuki listened intently in silence.

'When I asked my mother if she would ever forgive me, she said: *When the people we love make mistakes, we must try to overcome them together.*' Kurihara chuckled in remembrance, her eyes crinkling behind the lenses of her glasses. 'She told me she wanted to share in my sorrow over my failures and mistakes. That she would listen to my reflections, face all problems by my side, and watch over me so that they would never happen again. Because she loved me. I was so, so happy.'

Oh what a good mother, thought Mizuki. Kurihara was clearly a child raised by wonderful parents.

Kurihara's gentle expression seemed strangely radiant as she spoke, and Mizuki felt a vague sense of wonder. In response, Kurihara laid her hand – one size smaller than Mizuki's – over her clenched fist, and gave it a timid squeeze.

'Mizuki, if you're feeling sorry about bullying anyone, then let's be sorry together. Let's agree to make sure it never happens again. Do you think that might work?'

Right here and now, this girl is offering to accept me as I am. Mizuki didn't know if she should feel glad or pathetic. This was the first time anyone had ever spoken to her like this. Could someone come along and so easily accept the ugliness that Mizuki herself was only just beginning to own up to, and even offer to share in it so simply? Could such a miracle happen?

'You really don't know anything about me,' said Mizuki. 'So don't be so quick to speak. You're bound to be disappointed someday.'

'*Disappointed* is a word people use when they only think they know somebody,' Kurihara said simply. 'Mr. Shōhei taught me that. People who think they know someone but don't really understand a person on the inside, people who only see what they assume, they're the ones who use words like that. *He was such a disappointment*, they'll say. But those who really see someone, those who know, they won't do that. You shouldn't sum up someone's actions with a label like that, he said. And I think so, too.'

Heat radiated from Kurihara's small palm, bathing Mizuki's hand in warmth.

'I decided then that I'd never use that word. Ever. So I won't say it now. Besides, I'm doing this because I want you as a friend. You can't disappoint me. I want us to really see each other – or, no, what I really want is for us both to make each other see. That's the kind of friendship I want.'

It was hot. Where their hands were touching, Mizuki's skin was damp with sweat. How was Kurihara able to say this so openly? If they swapped places, Mizuki would be too embarrassed to say a word of that to anyone ever, but especially to a classmate. What if the person burst out laughing and started to make fun of her? The thought hung in her mind, but, ultimately, Mizuki decided it made her happy. Happy that someone wanted to know her this way.

'Okay. But you should know that I've been acting kind of high and mighty, like royalty,' Mizuki said in a small voice. Kurihara looked at her, waiting. 'That might be my nature. I didn't think of myself that way, but now I realise I really do have that in me. I'd like to change that. Still, you might catch me acting bossy or saying something that bothers you, sometimes. If you do . . .'

'You want me to tell you?' Kurihara responded quickly. 'That's fine with me. In fact, it's my speciality!' She sounded happy. 'I'm always saying things like that to people. In fact, sometimes I have trouble holding back. So I don't think I'll have to worry about you bossing me around. Right then, what do you say? Will you be my friend?' Kurihara jerked a thumb cockily towards herself. 'I think it would be a lot of fun!'

Mizuki could only stare at her in wonder. Who was this girl who would speak with raw emotion one moment and then joke around like that the other? Mizuki had never seen anyone who was in such a constant state of change.

'Uh-oh. Did I get it wrong? Mr Tsugi said it was important to be positive, but . . .' Kurihara's expression changed in a flash.

Seeing her look of confusion, Mizuki burst into involuntary laughter.

'I was just surprised!' Mizuki giggled. 'Nobody has ever asked me to be friends this way. But, well, it's very nice to meet you . . . Shima.'

Kurihara's eyes widened as Mizuki used her given name for the second time, and then she smiled as if a great weight had been suddenly lifted from her. The eyes behind the lenses of her pink glasses formed a pair of merry arcs.

'Yes! I'm so happy! Finally, I scored a friend!'

'Let's be good friends!' Mizuki said.

It sounded just like a conversation between two kindergarten students. But maybe it was for the best, Mizuki thought, to build a friendship starting from square one like this. She could learn all over again how to get along with others. That would be a good thing.

'Well, then, let's go and find a café somewhere and kick off the new friendship with a toast, okay?'

'Don't be silly, we have to go back to school! We're not allowed to take off without an excuse – I mean, we could be marked absent!'

Mizuki suddenly felt able to make the trip to school that had seemed next to impossible that morning, and to return to the classroom that she had wanted so badly to escape earlier. It would all be okay. She was sure now that she'd make it, even among Erina and her friends. Mizuki only needed to remember what a bully she herself had been, and the courage of the girls who had stood up to her. And that Shima had accepted her despite all that.

'Aww, but the café . . .?'

'Okay, that's enough. We're going back!'

Mizuki took Shima's hand, and they rose together. Feeling the reassuring warmth there, they ran off.

After dinner, Mizuki pulled out a pair of cream soda parfaits that Shima had recommended from the Tenderness summer dessert line.

'What's this?' her mother said. 'A convenience-store dessert? That's a surprise.'

'I thought it would be nice to have treats together, once in a while.'

The plastic cup was filled with bright blue, cream-soda-flavoured jelly, with a white jelly cloud floating right in the middle. It was decorated with fresh whipped cream and grapefruit on top, with a chocolate penguin mother and chick perched together among the snowy whipped-cream mountains.

Mizuki's mother removed the lid. 'Oh, it's really very cute!' she exclaimed, sounding impressed. 'Convenience-store sweets have come a long way, haven't they!' After a pause, Sumie chuckled and said, 'So, then, to what do I owe the pleasure? Was there something you wanted, perhaps?'

'Well, actually,' Mizuki replied, 'there was something I wanted to ask you.'

'Another surprise. What do you need? Clothes? Shoes? A bag?'

'I think you and Dad should get a divorce.'

Sumie's smile froze on her face.

Mizuki continued, carefully. 'I'm grateful for the financial support he sends, and I hope he keeps doing that. I was just thinking, maybe it would be good to let him have the divorce, for the sake of that other child.'

Just as her father no longer seemed to consider Mizuki his darling daughter, she no longer yearned for his presence in her life. She appreciated his concern for her well-being, but if he didn't need to be there, she didn't need to beg him. If there was another child that needed that more, it didn't matter to Mizuki whether he was legally bound to her or not.

'I don't need a father for emotional support. I have you, Mother, and that's more than enough. Of course I think that what you've been telling him was right. I know you refused the divorce for my sake, that you were just trying to be strong for me.'

Would her mother understand? Mizuki tried desperately to put her thoughts into words.

'But if doing the right thing means that someone else suffers or gets hurt, I think maybe it's okay not to insist on what's right. That's why I think you should let him have the divorce.'

Sumie gazed at Mizuki. Time seemed to pause as she looked at her daughter.

'What made you think of such a thing?' Sumie asked.

'It's hard to explain,' Mizuki said, and hesitated. 'But it's because I learned about the power that comes with being right, and the arrogance that can come with that power. And then, even more than that, I was thinking about two plastic tea bottles of kindness someone gave me. I thought maybe the person who needed them most was that other child.'

The two bottles that Old Red had given her. She was supposed to share that kindness. Old Red had said the two bottles were for Shima, but Mizuki couldn't use them for that anymore. When she wondered if there was anyone else who needed them instead, the child her father had called 'Tatsuki' came to mind. She wasn't sure whether that was two bottles' worth of kindness. But she definitely wanted to do something. She wanted to pay it forward.

Mizuki and Sumie sat at the table, with the two desserts laid out between them. By the side of a blue soda sea, a penguin mother and daughter nestled sweetly together.

Epilogue

She possessed a delicate, almost dreamlike beauty.

The door chime announcing a new customer rang out, and Tarō Hirose looked up from arranging the fried items behind the checkout counter.

'Welcome to . . . er . . .'

He couldn't look away.

Curls of lovely chestnut hair, skin so pure white it was almost translucent. Eyes, nose and everything perfectly proportioned on a doll-like face. A slender and graceful body, clothed in what looked to be a most elegant suit.

Tarō was used to beautiful people. He spent much of his time hanging around with a man who was like a nymph sprung from a fountain of pheromones. In addition, many customers came to the store with their sights set on the manager, beautiful men and women, perfectly turned out, trying to look their best. To put it bluntly: when it came to your everyday beautiful people, Tarō had seen it all before.

But now, at this moment, his eyes were riveted. Who *was* this person?

When the woman noticed Tarō looking her way, she smiled softly. She looked to be in her late twenties, but the girlish appearance of her face gave him a real jolt.

'Wow, she's gorgeous.' Mitsuri Nakao, who shared Tarō's shift, gave a low whistle. She looked at the woman with eyes shining. 'She's a first-time customer. If I'd seen her before, I would definitely have remembered.'

'Yeah. She looks so sophisticated, somehow.'

'Doesn't she? She'd give Jewel a run for her money,' Mitsuri said.

'You think so?' Tarō replied. Everything about Jewel was overwhelmingly beautiful. Her all-around perfection was hard to match. This customer was gorgeous, certainly, but anyone would have to admit that she wasn't quite up to Jewel's standard. Still, even Jewel had never held his gaze like this. 'I don't know,' he said. 'Somehow it feels wrong to compare them.'

'Oh really?'

While they were talking, the woman had drifted over to the books and magazines section, out of view from the checkout counter.

'I can't quite put my finger on it somehow,' he continued, 'but she has something that Jewel doesn't, like they'd be competing on different battlefields. I don't know, I just have a really funny feeling about her.'

Pffft! Mitsuri made a strange, muffled snort. When Tarō looked at her in concern, she started to giggle and gave him a knowing look. 'She's definitely your type. A delicate flower, right? That's what turns you on.'

'What?!' Instantly, Tarō's face went red.

'You know, fragile but sensual, looks like she just stepped out of a painting by Yumeji Takehisa. Slender as a girl, but with the aura of a grown woman.'

'Now wait . . . That's going too far!'

Was that his type? No way. But, then again, every one of the pop stars and actresses that he used to obsess over might have matched that description, more or less.

His previous girlfriend, Tsubaki, had been on the full-figured side, if anything. She looked good in trendy make-up, not a classical beauty in any sense, but he hadn't been attracted to her for her looks, particularly. From the beginning, he had never really been into categorising women as 'his type' or not. But once it was called out like that, examples came flooding back to him, and before he knew it he was blushing. It was horribly embarrassing to have one's own unrecognised sexual preferences pointed out by another person – especially by a senior work colleague about the same age as his parents!

'Ugh, no . . . can you just . . .'

'It's fine, it's fine! I promise I won't tell anyone. Besides, the people you're drawn to aren't necessarily the ones you end up loving. After all, my eternal crush will always be Leonardo DiCaprio during his *Romeo + Juliet* phase.' She nodded to herself a couple of times, then added, 'But I guess young men today really go for that sweet, seductive look, don't they? Ack! I sound just like an old lady, don't I?'

'What? Okay, enough already!'

As Mitsuri nattered on, Tarō managed to collect himself somewhat.

He took another look at the young woman, who had moved on to the beverage aisle. She didn't seem to be in any particular hurry, just browsing through the various store offerings, one by one. He could see her slender fingers tracing the labels on the bottles of tea.

Okay, well, so that's my type. I guess it's good to know. Makes sense, I suppose.

Tarō wasn't even sure he understood what made sense, but it was astonishing all the same. It was unbelievable that after all these years alive he didn't know his own preferences. Or maybe it was just strange to have those preferences walk through the door as a living, breathing woman.

'Well, anyway . . . maybe I'm just a shallow guy. All about looks?'

'What, are you going all introspective on me, now?' Mitsuri chuckled softly, then her voice lifted. 'Oh! Hello, Jewel. You're in casual wear. Not working today?'

'Yes, that's right. I was watching a TV drama last night until all hours, and I just woke up.'

Jewel had come in through the door to the dine-in space. She was dressed in a T-shirt and long shorts, her hair tied into a loose bun atop her head. He could still see the impressions the bedclothes had made on her cheek.

'My brother left me on my own. He took off in a bus with the fan-club ladies. They're going on a day trip, so I thought I'd keep watching the show while I ate. I'm gonna binge the whole series! Oh! Hirose, do you want to watch it with me? I can wait until you're done at work. It's the zombie one, it's so freaky!'

'Not me.'

'What, are you scared, maybe?' Jewel laughed.

Her face without make-up looked innocent, as if she were still a high-school student. Looking at that pristine smile, Tarō wondered whether the girl understood the risks of inviting a man his age to be alone with her in her room. Did she let her guard down because she thought of him as safe? No, probably she just hadn't given the matter any thought whatsoever.

'They're just television zombies, anyway. Not scary at all.'

'If you say so . . .'

Jewel laughed out loud. She was undeniably adorable, Tarō thought. But she didn't hold his gaze the way that other customer did. It was strange. What was the difference between Jewel and the other woman?

As if she could read Tarō's mind, Mitsuri said, 'Jewel will figure it out eventually. If someone with those looks knew how to flirt like that at her age, that would be a whole lot scarier than zombies.' Mitsuri glanced briefly towards the beverage aisle, adding, 'That one certainly knows, that's all I'm saying.'

Tarō was dumbstruck. He had known Mitsuri for a long time, but her remarkable intuition and keen powers of observation continued to amaze him. Speaking of which, she had apparently known the manager and Tsugi were related long before he himself did. How could she be so in touch with everything that happened at the store?

'What are you two talking about? Something scarier than zombies?' Jewel asked innocently. 'Let's watch it.'

Mitsuri smiled in reply. 'No, nothing important. Tell me about your TV drama, was it that good? It's the one everyone's talking about, right? Should I watch it too?'

'Yes, you totally should! It's all I can think about. I was even thinking of asking my brother Mitsu to get me a crossbow for my birthday.'

'A crossbow? What would you do with something like that?'

'Well, Tsugi gets work in the mountains sometimes, so I could go with him, maybe, and take the crossbow? Things like that.'

'Oh dear! I can just about imagine Tsugi coming home with an arrow sticking out of him.'

The two of them started to banter cheerfully. Tarō was watching them when an excited voice broke in: 'Is that my little Jewel?! I can't believe it. What are you doing here? It's been so long, hasn't it? Do you remember me?'

The gorgeous customer had finally made her way from the beverage aisle to the checkout counter.

'I'm just delighted to run into you!' she added, cheeks flushing rose red. She seized Jewel's arm. 'It's me. Hana Kanzaki. You know, I was with your brother Tsugi.'

'Let go of me.' Jewel, whose smile had vanished, wrenched her arm from the woman's grasp. Her face had frozen and she took a step back. 'Why are you here! I don't believe it. Didn't I tell you I hated you? I never want to see you again!'

'Now, really. Are you still angry, little Jewel?'

The woman named Kanzaki laughed softly. It was an indulgent laugh, the kind you'd use when confronted with a petulant child. But that only added fuel to Jewel's fire.

'Angry? I hate you! I'll never forgive you for what you did to Tsugi!'

'Never forgive me, you say? I would think you'd want to thank me, instead.'

'That will never happen!' As she spoke, Jewel gave Kanzaki a shove. 'Get out! Get out of here! This is my special place!'

The doorbell melody played again. Tarō, who had been standing by, stunned, turned to look. A man in a tailored shirt and chino pants poked his head into the store. Behind him, they could see a red Alfa Romeo sportscar.

'Hana, honey, are you ready? That's a long time for a bottle of tea. Is something wrong?'

'Oh, sorry! I ran into an old acquaintance.' Kanzaki spoke sweetly, as if nothing out of the ordinary had happened, then turned back to Jewel. 'I apologise, dear. Clearly it was too much of a shock for you, our running into each other so suddenly. But I'm glad we did. Because if you're here, it means I'll surely have a chance to see Tsugi again.'

'Why would you do that? You just can't!' Jewel snapped. But Kanzaki just laughed softly.

'Would Tsugi agree with you, I wonder? After all, a little sister can't possibly understand what happens between a man and a woman, can she?'

Her voice had dropped to a low whisper, and the corners of her mouth curled gently. The woman's smile sent a shiver down Tarō's spine. It was a chill of fear, as if he'd discovered that a beautiful flower he'd been admiring was actually dripping with deadly poison.

'Tsugi wouldn't . . . Tsugi—'

'I think we've heard enough about you and your brother.' Kanzaki ran a gentle hand down Jewel's cheek, still flushed with anger. 'I'll be back,' she said, and spun on her heel.

Kanzaki turned lightly towards the man.

'Darling, sorry to keep you waiting. I'm done here, so let's go. Oh, and they don't carry the tea that I like. Can we try another place?'

The man responded with an easy-going smile. 'Of course. But, Hana, I doubt we'll find your cup of tea at a convenience store.'

'We'll find it eventually. After all, there are convenience stores everywhere.'

The two left the store, and the automatic doors closed slowly behind them.

'Who was that woman?' Mitsuri was the first to open her mouth. 'There was something utterly wicked about her.'

Tarō and Mitsuri looked at Jewel. Glaring at the Alfa Romeo as it pulled slowly from the car park, she spoke through clenched teeth. 'Someone who hurt Tsugi,' she said. 'Because of her, Tsugi . . . Tsugi lost someone he loved.'

Mitsuri gasped, and Tarō felt his heart skip a beat.

It seemed the woman wasn't just beautiful, she was also dangerous. And she was clearly planning to return to the store.

Who knew what would happen next at the Golden Villa Tenderness in Koganemura?

Credits

Sonoko Machida and Orion Fiction would like to thank everyone at Orion who worked on the publication of *Meet Me at the Convenience Store by the Sea*.

Editor
Rhea Kurien

Copy-editor
Jade Craddock

Proofreader
Francine Brody

Editorial Management
Niyati Naudiyal
Jane Hughes
Charlie Panayiotou
Lucy Bilton
Patrice Nelson

Audio
Paul Stark
Louise Richardson
Georgina Cutler-Ross

Contracts
Rachel Monte
Ellie Bowker
Phoebe Miller

Design
Loveday May
Ola Galewicz
Nick Shah
Deborah Francois
Helen Ewing

Photo Shoots & Image Research
Natalie Dawkins

Finance
Nick Gibson
Jasdip Nandra
Sue Baker
Tom Costello

Inventory
Jo Jacobs
Erika Andrejuskinaite

Production
Ruth Sharvell
Katie Horrocks

Marketing
Holly Wilson

Publicity
Kate Moreton

Sales
Dave Murphy
Victoria Laws
Sammy Luton
Group Sales teams across Digital, Field, International and Non-Trade

Operations
Group Sales Operations team

Rights
Rebecca Folland
Tara Hiatt
Ruth Case-Green
Maddie Stephenson
Ruth Blakemore
Marie Matuschka

RAISING READERS
Books Build Bright Futures

Dear Reader,

We'd love your attention for one more page to tell you about the crisis in children's reading, and what we can all do.

Studies have shown that reading for fun is the **single biggest predictor of a child's future life chances** – more than family circumstance, parents' educational background or income. It improves academic results, mental health, wealth, communication skills, ambition and happiness.[1]

The number of children reading for fun is in rapid decline. Young people have a lot of competition for their time. In 2024, 1 in 10 children and young people in the UK aged 5 to 18 did not own a single book at home.[2]

Hachette works extensively with schools, libraries and literacy charities, but here are some ways we can all raise more readers:

- Reading to children for just 10 minutes a day makes a difference
- Don't give up if children aren't regular readers – there will be books for them!
- Visit bookshops and libraries to get recommendations
- Encourage them to listen to audiobooks
- Support school libraries
- Give books as gifts

There's a lot more information about how to encourage children to read on our website: **www.RaisingReaders.co.uk**

Thank you for reading.

---

[1] OECD, '21st-Century Readers: Developing Literacy Skills in a Digital World', 2021, https://www.oecd.org/en/publications/21st-century-readers_a83d84cb-en.html

[2] National Literacy Trust, 'Book Ownership in 2024', November 2024, https://literacytrust.org.uk/research-services/research-reports/book-ownership-in-2024